MW01123079

EWBERLIN

Hans Joachim
Schaedlich

EWBERLIN

Translated by Hans Werner

Hans Joachim

Schaedlich

EWBERLIN

Translated by Hans Werner

TORONTO
Exile Editions
1992

First published by Rowohlt Verlag GmbH, Reinebeck bei Hamburg, 1987

This edition is published by Exile Editions Ltd.,
20 Dale Avenue, Toronto, Canada
M4W 1K4

Sales distribution
General Publishing Co. Ltd.,
30 Les Mill Road, Don Mills, Ontario, M3B 2T6

Designed by MICHAEL CALLAGHAN
Printed by BEST GAGNÉ

ISBN 1-55096-0083

The publisher wishes to acknowledge the assistance towards publication of the Ontario Arts Council

CONTENTS

IN THE PROVINCES

In a remote but scenic province, in a city the Governor has chosen for his capital because there are enough buildings in it, it's always raining when the sun should be shining.

The Governor's ill-humour first thing in the morning comes from the view outside his window. The square in front of the official residence is filled with puddles. Puddles mirroring puddles. And there's no one to complain to, that that's how it is.

The Governor dresses himself without assistance in order to be spared the usual chatter and news of the day before breakfast. He doesn't bother to put on a dressing gown. He hasn't yet decided whether he'll have breakfast alone too; that is, except for those who serve him and then discreetly withdraw.

But he can't get it out of his head, either, that he really wants to hear what he doesn't want to hear. So breakfast with his adviser, who reads him the news from a portfolio.

The day before yesterday, that there won't be enough corn for the King if there's going to be any left for the peasants. Yesterday, that the peasants, because they don't have enough corn, are letting it rot. And today, just as the

Governor is swallowing his first bite, that certain writers, the usual authors, are kicking up a fuss.

What are they clamouring about?

They don't want to do as they're told. And have the cheek to say, because the Governor demands silence that's all the more reason to speak out.

About what?

That the Governor's reasons are only the Governor's reasons.

The Governor jumps up, leaving his breakfast unfinished.

What's to be done with them? asks the adviser.

What's to be done? says the Governor. I'll feed some of them so they'll sing to my tune. For others, I'll put my foot down. The rest, I'll kick their heads in.

(1978)

BUT SOMEONE

A building, long and high, but not too high among the surrounding buildings, its corridors inhabited by people from the neighbouring country, whose presence is tolerated in the city even though no one from the city is supposed to go into the building. The police walking up and down in front of the building, or rather one sitting in a glass booth and the other standing at the entrance, are there only to protect the building. Anyone goes in, they look him over; anyone comes out, they look him over. Plain to see for anyone who's going in, so he goes in without any *special* misgivings about the police, and re-emerges after the inevitable interval as someone from the city who has talked to the people from the neighbouring country who just happen to speak the same language he does. Has gone into the building therefore, and is free to go on his way anyway. Which comes as a surprise to anyone who knows that nobody from the city is supposed to go into the building.

Who, however, protects the people from the building? No one has ever actually said that a citizen is forbidden to go into the building. But he's not supposed to. He sees the policemen who see him as he's coming out, takes three hesitant steps from the entrance to the curb, waits for the car passing from left to right towards the main thoroughfare, and crosses the street. Hurrying to the corner, he turns left into the main street and takes a little time to look at a display of tobacco pipes in a shopwindow. Actually, he wants to take a quick look back to where he's just come from. Except for the pedestrians on the sidewalk, all he sees are the rows of buildings on the main street, not the building he's just left around the corner on the sidestreet. *He* can't see the entrance to the building, nor can anyone else standing here.

But someone standing behind him has seen it and also him, coming out of the building, and some one else, just the policeman who *usually* stands here, sees something, but the citizen sees neither the one nor the other who's practically standing inside a delivery entrance. He stops looking at the shopwindow and continues along the sidewalk. When he's already gone far enough to have forgotten all about the building he's just come out of, a policeman appears on the sidewalk and waits casually, keeping half an eye on the citizen coming towards him.

From the stream of pedestrians the policeman singles out the the citizen who came out of the building on the sidestreet. He raises his right hand to his visor, the way he learned at the police academy, identifies himself and demands to see the citizen's ID. What for? Unstated: for the better maintenance of public order you may be required to produce your ID on demand, which is reason enough. Only the policeman says it differently, as one who's got the right. He reads out the citizen's name, loudly. He reads it out a second time, loudly. And a third. Loudly.

And where might the citizen live? The citizen tells him and the policeman says, Oh, *there*, eh? Well, let's just see if you're right, and pages through the passbook, where the address is entered just as the citizen said. Just happens you're right, says the policeman.

Just happens? says the citizen. What do you mean...

Just happens, I said! says the policeman.

There's an ID-photo too. *That's* supposed to be you? says the policeman. Got your hair cut, eh?

The citizen searches along the direction of the policeman's gaze but still can't see the building he came out of, and, preoccupied and at a complete loss, asks whether he needs an affadavit from his barber too.

The policeman is sure of it. A picture like *that,* and somebody like *you* yet, call that ID, anybody's, that's no ID.

The citizen doesn't notice that the policeman has seen something. Someone behind the citizen, raising a hand to check the part in his hair, stopping in mid-gesture and at shoulder height to point to a citizen, so fast, it's all part of a single motion, nothing special in the universal desire to look presentable in public. Which is why the citizen is standing helplessly in front of the policeman.

Is it really necessary to describe the building, its location, who's in it? To name names? Such-and-such a city, such-and-such a street, the main street, the sidestreet? The citizen? Names. Words, phrases: phrases, words. Isn't it all interchangeable? A hand laid on someone by someone listening; someone listening handed over. Enough of a difference to tell them apart?

(1978)

PARTICULARS

Two motorists—reason for journey may be taken for granted—plus two additional persons, underaged and therefore not able to be named as motorists but only as minors in the accompaniment of the motorists; four persons in all, standing in a close relationship to one another which states the two older persons to be man and wife and the two younger, daughters—and daughters of the man and wife moreover—are climbing into a medium-size Russian-built car that bears a considerable resemblance to a certain Mediterranean model. Since they are inclined to travel in good old gypsy style, the car has previously been loaded down with all feasible requisites of clothes and shoes, food and toys. And for a very good reason. The motorists are not to be deterred by the worst roads and the deepest vallies, and must be fully equipped for an isolation of unknown duration. A cat (colour: black) is required to complete the picture as a fifth occupant entrusted to the minors to amuse themselves with in accordance with former practice.

The apartment they have left behind is completely bare. A scrap of paper, perhaps, lies in the corner of the largest room at the front where a hawthorn bush outside the window interrupts the view of a street which is said to have a special relationship to minors in fairy tales.[1]

Nor should their departure be passed over in silence.

The sky, incidentally, is grey, the low temperature more appropriate to last month. Even thick icey drops are falling.

Before they get to a road leading out into the country they must cross the city which, from their long stay there, is so well-engraved on the motorists' minds that the sight of it automatically assumes an aspect of permanence.

On the road heading mile upon mile in a northwestly direction towards a scenic destination, they feel light as air. They do not, however, plunge down a steep ravine, but keep going. And going. And going.

With the evening the road straightens out, the motorists' silence is their conversation. The minors, using the cat as a conversation piece, bicker over what it's saying. They eat all the buns and drink all there is to drink. According to the plans of the motorists, for whom the road leads ineluctably in the direction of irrevocable departure, the minors should be getting sleepy. But they wake up.

The car stops on a washed-out stretch of deserted road miles from any city or village. In total darkness the man and wife take daughter, cat and daughter into a field.

The cat, upset by the timid curiosity of the minors, jumps out of their arms and, black, hides itself in the field.

---

1 German fairy tales frequently begin with: Once upon a time there were two little children that lived on a street....

—*Translator's note.*

Time to get out of here. The minors, locked into the narrower confines of the car with promises they don't believe, make up for the loss by bickering.

There should have been fields, pastures and woods on either side, but only the trees lining the road are visible, and the grass between the trees. And a house, announcing the presence of a village. Before they reach the houses someone steps out towards them. The vehicle, ordered to the side of the road, is defective, says the officer, plain to see what the problem is, even in the dark. The headlight's out. It's night, so the damage must be repaired on the spot, but it's also night on the side of the road, so the damage can't be repaired on the spot.

The vehicle's prescribed destination for the first day is set down in a document the motorist (male) shows the officer who must comply with the provisions of the travel permit as well as the rules of the road. To wit, that the vehicle, having a faulty headlight, cannot now proceed to its prescribed destination by the end of the first day; that, however, it is supposed to proceed, and must proceed, to its prescribed destination by the end of the first day. The officer says all the right things to the motorist and the motorist says all the right things to the officer, the one as helpless as the other.

The officer's officer must be consulted, who says, Let him go then. The officer says, Alright, you can go then.

But only as far as a nearby town where the vehicle must be made roadworthy.

In the town where the motorists would have found rest before the next-to-last stage of their journey, thought of the next-to-last stage of their journey leaves them no rest. Almost all the time is spent in making repairs to the car.

The motorists and the minors, wide-awake from fatigue, and the car, driven all-out in a final push to their goal, are coming up to where the country ends. But something's gone wrong with the car again; this time, unlike the last, you can hear it. The car is losing speed, how are they supposed to make it in the short hour they have left. No stopovers on said territory are contemplated for said motorists after expiration of said time.

A car alone on a dark road, limping along towards a place lit up by bright lights in a desolate landscape.

The motorists' eyes do not notice the metallic structures, are drawn instead to the only thing moving in the empty light. One of the daughters, not seeing the armed guard she expected, does not notice the guard is armed and assures him he is loveable.

As for the guard, he merely expects the motorists not to have made a mistake. He is only authorized to see if they are entitled to proceed to another check-point which is, however, *maximally* authorized. But if the motorists really have made a mistake, he'd know what to do.

Previously unknown to the motorists, and not especially useful information later, but vaguely noticed during the course of the last few minutes, they are searching for something in the gas tank— which contains gas— and are looking for somebody under the seat the minors are sitting on— but the cat is long gone in the field— and are doing a lot of paperwork handed to them by the motorists. A paper is collected from each of the occupants and retained, and, after a head-count, man and wife and daughter and daughter roll out into the darkness in a broken-down car, not knowing where the country they can't see ends on the road between one country and the next. No white line. Not a sound.

More lights and signs, only the name of the country they have just come from is different on these signs. That's the *other* country, the man and wife say.

One of the daughters, noticing the guard is carrying a weapon strapped across his chest, asks why the guard is armed, and, because this guard remains silent too, answers herself with a question. An explanation from the wife, however, refers to Indian territory further up-country, leaving it open as to direction. The guard must request them to produce the many papers, which they have just shown him, for closer inspection, and to enter the names of the man and wife, the daughter and daughter, their place of origin and destination into a log-book.

The last stretch of the flat road, which the guard has shown them in two sections—the first easily, the second barely, recognizable—on the map, looms up ahead of the car which is gradually running down.

Still, but only just, the car finds its way easily to the metropolis, though the noise of the malfunction is conspicuously loud. Nevertheless the minors are asleep and do not wake up when the car rolls to a halt.

Two motorists, in addition to two underaged persons and all their clothing and shoes, no food however, but lots of toys, will just have to get themselves from here to an establishment in the north whose sturdy timbered construction has permitted it to withstand the ravages of time.

Picked up with all their belongings by a strange car that tears pluckily along under a nation-wide rainstorm, man, wife, daughter and daughter at last arrive at a destination which offers many a rich opportunity for poetic contemplation.

(1978)

TIGHTROPE

P., who does a daily tightrope-walk between two towers high over the heads of the crowd—a lane is kept clear beneath him—is listening to a proposal from the entertainment committee.

You're too high up for the spectators to follow you step by step. They, on the ground, should see what you see in the air. So you will speak as you walk. The spectators in the square will hear it over a loudspeaker. But you will not be alone. Even you will hear something, namely what I tell you. The spectators will hear it too, and that will complete the effect for everyone on the ground.

P. hesitates. In fact, he often talks to himself on his walk across the rope. But it's nothing to tell others about. Mostly he just gives himself advice.

It'll be easy for you, says Z. Don't worry about it. Just talk to yourself. Anything. Every word the spectators hear is a word snatched from the jaws of death. That's good enough.

P. accepts the proposal. It's almost time for his performance anyway. He tests the fit of his shoes and looks up in the sky for signs of rain.

He puts his right foot on the rope. The spectators spot him.

Z. shouts in his ear, Why don't you say something?

I am placing my left foot on the rope, I see the city, how small it looks, says P. I can't see any faces. I place my right foot in front of my left. I have to remind myself that everything I see matters. The order of the streets and houses, the movements of the spectators. The rope is mildewed. I have to take that into consideration.

Are you afraid? shouts Z.

Yes, but I'm taking another step before it gets any worse.

What do you see? shouts Z.

I see ice-crystals. They're melting. They're splashing on my face. The ones that don't hit me are falling on you. I'm slowing down. The rope is slippery.

Keep going, shouts Z.

The wind is disorienting, says P.

It's calm down here, says Z.

It's in my back, pushing me forward. I can't keep up with it.

Try, says Z. You can do it.

My feet are shaky, says P. I've got to stop.

Don't, shouts Z. You'll waste your strength. Keep your eye on the other end.

My hands are getting numb, says P.

Think of the spectators, shouts Z. They're behind you all the way.

I'm going on, says P.

You have no choice, shouts Z.

I'll go at a trot, says P. Speed helps.

I've missed the rope, P. yells. I'm falling off. I no longer think of the wind and the rain. But I see the clouds. I can see the cobblestones of the lane quite clearly. I've hit the ground! My head is split open. My arms and legs are broken. My body is bleeding.

What's he telling us all that for, the spectators ask, when we can see it for ourselves?

(1978)

TREES, GRASS, AND A RIVER

Any concern for outward appearances must have been furthest from his mind. It was not in his nature. Nor was any thought of whether the same look might justifiably be called a different look under different circumstances. Such that, had he assumed, or been at all able to assume, that his look was drawing attention to itself from all sides, or had, alternatively, been met with complete equanimity; whether, in the first instance, he would be imagining the hidden expression of sinister menace, or, in the second, would, after momentary bewilderment, only be describing what was in fact there.

He had no conception of his exterior at all, apart from rare glimpses in puddles, where he saw himself as no different from any of the others he saw daily.

Waking at the crack of dawn he set out across the meadow, oblivious to the sheaves of grass he was trampling down and to the animals peering out at him, or singing, apparently. He was as indifferent to rain as to sunshine, having no conception of either. Whether it was warm or cold was, however, a matter of some importance. He spent a long time down by the river, till noon, at least on a day like this. He just sat there, or lay on the ground. Mostly he lay on the ground. If he was lying under a tree he got caught up in the motion of the branches above his head, till, after some hours' time, he'd be rocking himself in the boughs.

He was spared any anxiety over his choice of words. But not over food and water. If he had none, he charged around, hunting until he found some. He slurped the water and munched the food, munched and slurped and slurped and munched; did not, however, save any that was left over.

From a distance he classed the people he met into the friendly and the unfriendly. It was not actually a considered appraisal—looks, gestures were equally meaningless— he was guided only by instinct, and not always infallibly.

The unfriendly, he avoided. Even so, they rarely came after him. In the early days he had often got into fights, had often won but come away with injuries. Latterly he merely stood his ground in the hope that his adversaries would back off. Only great skill enabled him to avoid further harm when they did not.

The friendly, he sought out. The fact that it didn't happen very often might have been something to reproach himself with, had his sort had any capacity for self-reproach. He and the friendly ones would sit together at various times of the day, twilight at the earliest. Their voices carried a fair distance, their games tore up the ground. Time went by, unnoticed. His time. Whether it was an easy time under the boughs or a hard time in the protracted hunt for food, he didn't know. All he knew was, he groaned when he was hurt, he yelped when they were playing their violent games; so that, like a guileless innocent perhaps, he had no conception of where day ended and night began. Night simply recurred again and again, at which times his constant companion was a curiosity that had something childlike about it, which distinguished it from mere stupidity. So he just stands there at the edge of the field, in mid-game, gaping at the sight of some strangers coming up. His instinct is blunted. Some of the others are also just standing there, some are running away. The strangers make a move in their direction, coming closer. Fight or play? Before he realizes it's fight, one of the strangers has thrown a net over him. In the net there's nothing to fight but the net. The more he struggles, the easier it is for the stranger to tighten the net. He is not the only one to be caught in the nets. The strangers talk to him, offer him strange food he's never seen before. At first he refuses it. They take him away in a van with the others.

Next morning, the van stops. The strangers release one of them from the net and let him out in an open field. Another before noon somewhere else, and a third at noon somewhere else again. He is the last. The strangers have to haul him out because he wants to stay in the net, in the van. They leave him in a place that only looks like the place he came from. Grass underfoot, trees just like trees. A river in the distance.

Again curiosity, more like absent-mindedness, drives him around in circles. The circle paced out, he's left with nothing but blades of grass trampled under his feet.

He bends over, sniffs the grass at his feet, and thinks he's seeing the grass that used to smell like the grass he's smelling now. He tears it up in clumps, grinds it between his teeth, spits it out, tears out more clumps of grass, throws them all over himself, throws himself into the grass, gives an agonizing howl, jumps up, chases over the field, still doesn't see the grass he's looking at, falls down at full gallop, rolls over, and churns up the ground, scraping up soil. He lies there, grunting out the rhythms of his panting breath. And falls asleep.

His hunger wakes him, he sees daylight, closes his eyes to shut out the light and holds his hands over his ears to shut out the sound of the wind and the rustling of the grass. Opens his eyes, sees the boughs of a tree, shuts his eyes and sees other boughs in another, more familiar, tree. Ears still tightly shut, he hears the wind in the boughs he sees behind his closed eyes. Their swaying motion bears him away. He falls asleep.

He wakes up in the dark. Feeling neither hunger nor thirst, he follows the smell of the river. This river is wider, with a strong current. For hours he runs along the bank. He stands at the river, staring out over the current. An echo follows his shouts. Nor does he drink from the river, as he might have. Till morning, he stands at the river. Just before dawn he closes his eyes and sinks down.

In his sleep he hears others who have sat by the river with him. He answers their calls. His call wakes him up. He calls after the others.

Weak from not eating, he's too weak to eat. He just lies there by the river. Rain is falling, but he sees the sun. He can't feel the cold.

Since there are still sounds coming out of him on the seventh day, he hears the strangers. But he does not open his eyes and is unable to move. They find him, pick him up and put him in their van. He is aware of the drive only as the memory of a drive in their van.The water they keep trying to pour down his throat spills over his teeth and streams down the sides of his face.

This drive is shorter. The strangers take him out of the van. Anxiously they lay him on a mat in a room with walls on three sides and open on the fourth, except for the bars across the opening.

He sees animals peering out at him, or hears animals singing, and opens his eyes. He sees the bars. A jug stands before him. Since he doesn't have to get up, he takes a drink. He doesn't touch the food beside the jug. But otherwise: no grass, no boughs, no river.

On the third day he has something to eat along with the water. Besides the food and the water he sees the strangers. But he does not sit up and remains wrapped in silence.

The strangers talk to him. He hears them without emotion. They bring others up to his room, whom they have caught in their nets. Touchingly, the others make the gestures he's familiar with. He, however, remains motionless. Rain, sun vanish. He has the fixed and vacant stare of an animal as he munches his food with the sounds of an animal eating, and slurps his water with the sounds of an animal drinking. In the middle of the room, on the edge of sleep, he just stands there in the sight of strangers coming up. Now that they're all waiting in vain for him to look at them, he conceals his look— which would in this case have been met with complete equanimity— behind his eyelids. The sign on the bars, which says he comes from such-and-such a place, is meant for his body. He is no longer waiting for anything.

(1979)

UNDER WAY

1. Ketzel goes astray

On the road, which was wide with an imperceptible rise, imperceptible at least to the eye—if not to the legs and feet—since numerous twists and turns obstructed the view as it rose through the city which had posted signs to the effect that the houses were inhabited by ARAG, Veedol and Pentax, and greeted him with faces that certainly looked like trustworthy faces, he fearlessly looked for the house he was to live in, and, much affected, did not find it.

2. Ketzel is silent

Supported on the arm of a friend he is still able to walk on a level path at the bottom of the valley, draws in his head, closes his eyes, hunches over, tries to be helpful by hauling his legs along with short steps, feet dragging along the ground the whole time, and hears the friend say that the mountain at the foot of the valley, a rocky mountain high as a thousand people, which is covered with snow, where the snow is white, where the sky above the mountain is boundless, where the sun above the sky is relentless, is nice.

3. Ketzel spills soup

At a table in the corner of the cafeteria, with Mr. Lumpkin sitting mid-way down it and complaining about having forgotten to have a hair-dryer for his wife installed along with the swimming pool in his home, Ketzel sits hunched over, holding a soup spoon with great difficulty, spoons up the soup that is supposed to be good for him, spills some on the way to his mouth, painstakingly unfolds the formidible napkin, wipes his chin, the waitress even smiles with forbearance, but Mr. Lumpkin, who owns a not yet fully appointed swimming pool, looks at Ketzel to see if he's bringing down the tone of the cafeteria where Mr. Lumpkin takes his meals.

4. Ketzel sallies forth

He is wearing brown shoes, dark brown pants, light brown shirt. A hundred metres uphill from the house is a forest. Between the house and the forest lies snow that has fallen during the night, is still falling, and is so deep that the top of the snow is higher than the top of his shoes. After two steps the snow gets into the brown shoes. After three steps snow lies on the shoulders of the light brown shirt. The left cuff of the dark brown pants was covered with snow after the first step, the right after the second. On his head Ketzel wears nothing but black hair which, like the shoulders of the shirt, also has snow lying on it after three steps. The snow stays on hair better than on skin, but after ten steps there is snow on his hands, which Ketzel does not put in pockets, on eyebrows, on nose, on cheeks, on mouth, chin, and ears. It will take Ketzel one hundred and fifty steps to cover the hundred metres of snow between house and forest. After twenty steps there is snow on the front of his shirt, on the back, and on the pantlegs from ankle to waist. The snow is falling vertically out of a cloud. After thirty steps the layer of snow on hair, shoulders, shirtfront, back, pantlegs, forehead, eyebrows, nose, cheeks, mouth, chin, and ears is, however, uneven. Some falls off the pantlegs. Some melts on forehead, nose, cheeks, mouth, chin, and ears. Some melts on hands, some falls off. After the fortieth step Ketzel licks the snow from his lips. Some melts on the shoulders and back of the shirt. After a third of the steps Ketzel needs to cover the distance, some of the melted snow on his forehead runs into his eyes. With his left hand Ketzel wipes the snow off the back of the right. With the back of the right, he wipes his eyes, right eye first. The coldness stings, bringing tears to his eyes, which mingle with the melted snow. Some snow has stayed on the back of the left hand. Fresh snow falls on the back of the right. After sixty steps some snow melts on the hairs in the back of his neck. It seeps between shirtcollar and neck. For the last few steps now, some of the snow that had fallen, and is still falling, into his shoes, has melted and is still melting. After seventy steps some melts into the black hair on his head. After eighty steps Ketzel, from above, looks white even though some of the snow has fallen, and is still falling, off him, and some of the snow has melted, and is still melting, on him. After ninety steps Ketzel feels cold because head, neck, shoulders, back, chest, arms, hands and feet are cold and wet from the melted snow, and also covered with freezing snow. True, Ketzel's head, neck, shoulders, back, chest, arms, hands and feet *feel* cold, but he *is* cold. After a hundred steps, which would have gotten Ketzel to the edge of the forest had they been metre-long steps, his whole body is white, except for the armpits. That is, face, insides of arms and legs, and the insides of the ears, are all white too, with the exception, still, of Ketzel's eyes, which are brown. After a hundred and two steps the snowfall is heavier than it was the whole hundred steps before. Many of the snowflakes are big as cherries, many, but not too many, are the size of rose-petals. All of them are like leaves falling. Snow, more snow, a lot of snow, has fallen on Ketzel's footprints. The footprints farthest behind him are completely filled in. The outlines are still visible, but only just. After a hundred and twenty steps Ketzel, now close to the forest, stops. He sees that there is hardly any or no snow under the dense growth of trees. He would like to run into the forest. There are only thirty steps to go. Snowflakes are falling in great numbers, but not like leaves anymore. They are falling fast, and, falling thick and fast on Ketzel, can no longer be told apart. The falling snow looks like the snow lying on the ground. Ketzel, all white with snow, is standing in the falling snow and in the snow lying on the ground. His footprints are all covered with snow, and Ketzel, standing in the snow, looks like a Ketzel lying in the snow.

(1979/1982)

ANOTHER DAY BEGINS

Four men live in the room. One of them is sitting on his bed, dressed, reading the paper. The front page. Another is lying on his bed, also dressed. Sleeping, maybe. A third, with his back to the room, is standing in front of his bedside table. He's chewing on something. A fourth, in his bathrobe, is sitting at the table, eyes closed, chin resting on his chest, hands clasped tight between his knees. He doesn't know who he is.

Miloslav is sitting on his bed. He is thirty years old. Weyrich is lying on his bed. He's thirty-seven. Strack is standing in front of his bedside table. He's seventy. Sitting at the table is Exter. He's forty-five.

The room has an area of twenty-nine point twenty-two square metres. It is an almost perfect square. Opposite the door is a window which almost takes up the entire width of the room. It is divided into three sections. The aisle from the door to the window is a little wider than the mid-section of the window. To the right and left of the aisle are two beds on each side, their headboards against the wall. To the right of each bed is a bedside table. The space between the beds is twice as wide as a bedside table. It is nine o'clock in the morning.

Weyrich gets up from his bed, takes cigarettes and lighter out of bedside table drawer, lights up, puts cigarettes and lighter on bedside table and goes into the small room projecting into the main room just to the right of the door. The small room has a toilet and sink.

The door to the small room is directly opposite the right window section. Between this door and the window there is room for Strack's bed and bedside table and Weyrich's bed and bedside table, with a space between the washroom door and Strack's bedside table, between Strack's bed and Weyrich's bedside table, between Weyrich's bed and the window section on the right.

Strack turns around. To the left of the main door stands a wardrobe with four partitions. Between the wardrobe and the window there is room for Miloslav's bed and bedside table and Exter's bed and bedside table and for a table and four chairs, with a space between the wardrobe and Miloslav's bed, between Miloslav's bedside table and Exter's bed, between Exter's bed and the table and four chairs, and between the table and four chairs and the window section on the left. The door to the small room with toilet and sink has a ventilation slit just off the floor.

Water is heard running into the sink for two or three seconds, and a noise. Something dropping into the plastic wastepaper basket. Weyrich comes out of the washroom, lies down on his bed. Strack takes cigarettes and lighter out of his bedside table and goes into the washroom.

The window faces east. The section on the left opens towards the left, the right towards the right, but only a crack. A short track that swivels outwards is fixed to the top of each window casement and attached to an angle-iron at the top of each of the window frames with a small padlock. The shackle of the padlock runs along the track for fifteen centimetres at most.

The room is on the third floor. Elevator and stairs lead up to the fourth. Other people live on the fourth floor, where the windows can be opened all the way.

Heard it from somebody who knows, says Exter. A guy from the third floor here, who went up to the fourth, took off his glasses, and folded them up in the corner of the windowsill for safekeeping. Then he climbed up on the windowsill, carefully, because he couldn't see too well without his glasses. Stepped right into thin air. He didn't have to go any further.

The floor is covered in green. The beds, except for wheels, endboards and headboards, are also green, but a paler green than the floor. The bedside tables are the same green as the beds and so are the lamps over the headboards.

Exter, in his bathrobe, goes out of the room, along the corridor to a hall, sits down at an unoccupied table, takes a pack of cigarettes and a lighter out of bathrobe pocket, and lights up. Two women are sitting at the next table, knitting. A man, still young, is walking back and forth in front of the tables. He puffs on a cigarette, inhales deeply, exhales noisily, puffs on the cigarette, inhales deeply and exhales, lips pursed the whole time. The two women at the next table are perhaps of an age. The dark-haired one looks bigger than the fair-haired one. The dark-haired one says, When he was drunk, he'd beat me. Always. And he drank practically every day. When he beat me, that's when he wanted it. Always. And there I was, pregnant for the second time. I didn't want to get beaten up anymore, I was six months gone already. He came home late, tore off the blanket and beat me. Starting with the face.

The man walking back and forth in front of the tables bursts out laughing.

I jumped out of bed, was going to lock myself in the kitchen, but I never got as far as the kitchen. He hit me on the head, on the back, tore open the apartment door and kicked me out. All I had on was a pair of panties. Middle of the night, half-naked, belly out to here. I rang on the neighbour's door, asked if I could stay there for the night.

The man stops at the table and bursts out laughing. He pulls the ashtray towards himself and keeps walking.

The child died. They'd put it in a foster home.

The man bursts out laughing, stops at the table, butts his cigarette and leaves.

It went to court. The woman put the blame on the man and the man put the blame on the woman.

Nothing much came out at the trial.

A map of the city hangs on the inside of the door. Subway lines and bus routes as they were in nineteen-seventy-six, complete with streetcar lines on the other side of the border. Accuracy, however, is only guaranteed for this side. No names are given for S-Bahn stations on either side. Smaller streets don't show up at all.

Exter comes back into the room. Miloslav, Weyrich and Strack are lying on their beds. Weyrich and Strack have their eyes closed. Miloslav is still reading the paper, but he's turned on his portable radio. Got to get dressed, says Exter. Yeah, says Weyrich. Miloslav says, The doctor's been round. Got to shave, says Exter. He sits on his pile of clothes lying on a chair to the left of the head of the table. He stares at the white tabletop with his head resting in his hands. Strack gets up and goes to the washroom.

A knock on the door. Nobody responds. Two dark-haired women in orange smocks come in. The younger one says, Djello. The older one says, Mornin, goes to the washroom door and opens it. Just a sec, shouts Strack, shutting it again. You oughta jist try gettin up in time, the woman shouts, Just a sec. The younger one, who has started to mop the floor, says something in her own language. The older one leaves.

A daily schedule hangs beside the map of the city. Morning exercises are over. Now it's time for activities. You coming, says Weyrich to Miloslav. In a minute, says Miloslav. Strack comes out of the washroom and says, Don't know what's wrong with me. Weyrich says to Strack, Why didn't you ask the doctor, before. Yeah, says Strack.

Got to get dressed, says Exter.

The older of the two dark-haired women comes back and goes into the washroom. Her orange gloves practically reach to her elbows. Briskly, she takes toothbrush mugs and soap-dishes down from the bracket, puts them on the back of the sink, gives the bracket a wipe and puts the soap-dishes back. One of the toothbrush mugs falls over, the toothbrush falls on the floor. She puts the toothbrush mugs back on the bracket, picks up the toothbrush, sticks it back into the mug, sprinkles the sink with a sharp-smelling cleanser, turns on the tap and rinses out the sink.

In the room the younger woman is pushing the chairs aside. Exter has to get up. He goes over to the window and leans up against the sill.

In the washroom the older woman lifts the toilet seat, cleans the bowl with a brush, flushes, knocks the brush out against the inside of the bowl, wipes the inside of the bowl, the top and bottom of the toilet seat, gets a rag, wipes the floor, and says, Where's alla them hairs comin from.

Weyrich and Miloslav go out. The two women go out. Strack lies down on his bed. Exter takes the chair he was sitting on before and pushes it under the table. Got to lie down, he says. Only I got to get dressed too.

It's pretty bad today, says Strack. Yeah, says Exter. Strack says, Could be the eyes maybe, on account of the glasses, but the doctor says no. I know, says Exter. Can't stop this shivering, says Strack. You don't see it, to look at a man. Yeah, says Exter. Strack says, Is it cold out? Don't know, says Exter. Strack says, Don't know why my legs are so heavy. The minute I lie down they go to sleep on me. Then my arms. Then me. In broad daylight. Never done that before. I keep thinking about what it was like before, what the garden looked like. Don't even know anymore. I shut my eyes and I see the garden. My wife's looking out of the window and I'm saying, Close the window, it's freezing. Everything's fine in the garden. Then I go into the house. Fits you like your own skin, a house, when you've been living in it for forty years. Same neighbours still living next door. That's what goes through my head. All day long. You knew this is where you belonged, no matter what.

Exter goes over to Miloslav's bedside table, turns off the radio. Used to like listening to music, he says. Before. He goes over to his own bedside table, takes cigarettes and lighter out of bathrobe pocket, lights a cigarette, puts the pack of cigarettes and lighter on bedside table, goes over to the window, which is open a crack, and, turning partly away from Strack, says, Not that I'm tired. But I'm not awake either. Hard to take for more than ten minutes a day, the first ten minutes in the morning when you wake up. Then the heaviness isn't so heavy, or no heavier than it's supposed to be. But once you're awake, it goes all dark and you're a stone. You don't get up, you don't wash, you don't get dressed. You don't eat and you don't drink. You don't want to see the tree in the yard, don't want to hear the voice in the tree either. The tree reminds you of another tree, the voice of another voice. Somewhere, where you're not. And here, where you are, there's this tree and this voice to remind you.

Strack says, Back then, when everything was going fine, a cigarette really used to taste good. Doesn't taste like much now. But I keep smoking because I'm thinking, Maybe if I keep smoking everything'll be alright again.

Strack speaks neither slowly nor softly, nor in a monotone. His voice is not hoarse. Exter speaks slowly, softly, and in a monotone. His voice is hoarse.

Exter goes into the washroom, holds the butt under the tap, turns on the water, turns off the water, throws the butt into the wastepaper basket, goes over to the table, opens his bathrobe, pulls his pyjama bottoms down below the knee with both hands, hauls his left leg out of the pyjama bottoms, loses his balance, lets the pyjama bottoms fall out of his hands, getting his feet caught in the waistband, and kicks the pyjama bottoms to the floor. Holding on to the edge of the right side of the table, he yanks his left leg out of the shapeless bundle, then his right, leans on the table, bends down, picks up the pyjama bottoms, lays them on the chair his clothes are lying on, picks up his underpants, and, with his back to the room, sits on the chair that is placed along the length of the table, pulls his underpants up over his knees, stands, and pulls them up the rest of the way. He takes off his bathrobe, lays it on his bed, picks up his undershirt, turns it rightside out, gathers it up under the collar, lifts it over his head, thrusts his head through the opening, then his arms through the armholes, right arm first, and pulls the undershirt down over his body with both hands. Picking up his shirt, unbuttoned, he holds it at shoulder height with his left hand on the right collar, pushes his right arm into the sleeve and pulls with the left hand till the collar is up beside his neck and the right hand emerges from the cuff, pushes the left arm into the sleeve till the left hand emerges from the cuff, and buttons the shirt up from top to bottom, leaving the the top button undone. Exter picks up his pants, climbs into the right pantleg, then the left, pulls up his pants, fastens them, zips them up, and tightens the belt. He sits on the bed, puts on his socks, stands up, steps into his shoes, sits on the chair, bends over and ties his shoelaces.

Weyrich comes in, says, Freezin in here, goes over to the window, shuts it, lies down on his bed, turns on his side and closes his eyes.

Miloslav comes in, goes over to his bedside table, turns on the radio, sits on the bed, opens the paper and says, Muggings and murder, nothing but murder and muggings. And ads.

The radio is giving a report on a national holiday from a station on the other side of the border. In Defence of the Fruits of the People's Labour.[1]

Weyrich says, You've got the class enemy on again. What do you mean, says Miloslav. Weyrich says, That's from the other side. So what, says Miloslav, So are you.

---

[1] This is a facetious combination of three common former East German slogans, trotted out on public occasions: In Defence of the Socialist Order (*Der Schutz der sozialistischen Gesellschaftsordnung*), The Fruits of Socialist Labour (*Die Früchte der sozialistischen Arbeit*), The Heroic Labour of the People (*Die heroische Arbeit des Volkes*). The reference to the "class enemy" is an ironic reversal of the fact that, on the other side of the Wall, West Germany was always referred to as such.
—*Translator's note.*

The nurse comes in, goes over to Weyrich and says, Time to take your blood pressure. She takes his blood pressure, gives him the result, goes over to the windowsill where a flower is standing in a pot, and says, My, whose lovely flower is this. Mine, says Exter. The nurse says, It could do with some water. Yeah, says Exter, only the water keeps leaking out. The nurse says, I'll get you a saucer. She goes out, comes back, sets the flower-pot on a saucer. Thanks, says Exter. What's the flower called, do you know? It's a poinsetta, says the nurse. Exter says, Bit early for Christmas, isn't it. Only seventeen more days, says the nurse and goes out.

Weyrich gets up off the bed, opens the drawer of his bedside table, takes out an apple, shuts the drawer, takes three bites out of the apple, chews them quickly, takes two bites out of the apple, chews them quickly, sticks the rest of the apple into his mouth and goes out, chewing.

Miloslav, Strack and Exter turn to the window. Exter says, It's snowing. Miloslav says, Snow. Noise of voices and steps in the corridor. The voices are faint, then louder. The rapid steps sound like sharp little heels. Strack says, That's Madame the Doctor.

Never any real snow around here, says Miloslav. Village where I come from, always had lots of snow there. My father had to shovel it first thing in the morning or we couldn't get out of the house. Says in the paper, wolves are already coming down into the village this year. People get the feeling it's going to be a long winter.

Weyrich comes in and says, There's a guy got up out of his chair in the hall there, suddenly looked all funny in the face and keeled over on the floor. Real hard. Face all blue, hands and feet shaking and him screaming, couple of times, then breaking out in a sweat. But people were already yelling for the doctor, who was there like a shot, and a nurse with her. Then somebody said, Bring the stretcher, which was already coming up anyway. I left because I didn't want to see any more. If I hadn't seen it with my own eyes. Somebody ought to write it down the minute something like that happens. Otherwise you don't know what it was like and nobody'll believe you.

Miloslav says, I believe you, if you say so. I don't have to see it. Or read about it. Besides, nobody can write it down the minute it happens. Put your watch on the table, and when it's nine o'clock, write, It's nine o'clock. Before you get the first word down, it's already a second after nine. When I read something like, It's nine o'clock, I already know something's fishy. Because you'd have to start writing before, at least a couple of seconds before, and stop on the dot of nine. Like on the radio, when they say, At the beginning of the long tone followed by ten seconds of silence. Or try writing that you're writing it down. As long as you're still writing it's not written down yet, and when it's all written down you're not writing anymore.

Weyrich says, But when I'm writing my wife a letter, and I write, Today is Sunday, so I'm writing you a letter, that's okay, isn't it.

Miloslav says, Yeah. But what if you don't finish the letter till Monday and don't say that Sunday's over already.

Strack says, Almost time for lunch. Weyrich says, What're we having today. Strack says, Cod with herb sauce and boiled potatoes.

Miloslav says, I like reading things where it says this or that was. Weyrich says, Don't matter to me if it's was or is. Main thing is, I know exactly what. Miloslav says, You only know that if you see it yourself. Or hear it. Exter is trying to say something. Yeah, he says, No. Then he goes out.

Exter comes back. Lunch, he says.

A knock. The door opens and Weyrich, Miloslav, Strack and Exter go to the door. A taciturn blond in blue smock and white cap is standing in front of a trolley with three open compartments. How many, she says. Weyrich says, Four. The woman hands him four knives, four forks, and gives Miloslav four mandarin oranges, Strack two bowls of salad and Exter two bowls of salad. Exter shuts the door with his elbow, goes over to the table where Weyrich has laid out the knives and forks, a knife and fork at each place, and Miloslav has put the oranges, in the middle, and Strack has set his two bowls of salad, one for Weyrich and one for Miloslav. Exter sets one bowl of salad on the table for Strack, and one for himself.

All four of them eat their salad at the same time. Exter eats his standing. Weyrich puts his empty bowl in the middle of the table beside the oranges. Miloslav puts his empty bowl inside Weyrich's bowl, Strack his inside Miloslav's, Exter his inside Strack's. They lay their forks down beside their knives. A knock. the door opens and a talkative brunette in blue smock, white apron and white cap says, Lunchtime. Come and get it.

There is a trolley in the corridor with hot food in sunken containers and in compartments underneath the containers. Weyrich, Miloslav, Strack and Exter go to the door. The woman says, How many potatoes today, Mr. Weyrich. Weyrich says, Not too many. The woman dishes potatoes out on a plate, a nurse on the other side of the trolley doles out a piece of fish, the woman ladles sauce over the potatoes, and says, There you are, Mr. Weyrich. And a yoghurt, says Weyrich. And a yoghurt, says the woman, And a dessert spoon for the yoghurt. Weyrich says, Thank you, and goes back to the table. The woman dishes potatoes out on a plate and says, That enough, Mr. Miloslav. Miloslav says, Yeah.

The woman says, There you are then, Mr. Miloslav. Strack says, Lots of potatoes. The woman says, Lots of potatoes. There you are, Mr. Strack, just for you, she says. Exter says, Just a regular portion. The woman says, Not too big and not too little. Enjoy your meal, Mr. Exter, she says. All four men say, Thanks. Exter shuts the door with his elbow and goes over to the table where three men are sitting and eating.

A knock on the door, the door opens and a nurse comes in carrying a tray on her right hand like a waiter. The tray has a rim and is divided into twenty-five little square compartments. A room number is written on the bottom of the first compartment in each row. The names of the occupants of each room are written on the bottoms of the rest of the compartments in each row, together with their medication and prescribed amounts for morning, noon and night. The medication is contained in little plastic cups sitting in the compartments with the names on them.

The nurse comes over to the table and says, Mr. Weyrich, handing him two small plastic cups. Weyrich shakes the contents of the one into his yoghurt, gives the little plastic cup, empty, back to the nurse, raises the second to his lips, knocks the pill back like a strong drink, swallows, gives the little plastic cup, empty, back to the nurse and goes on eating. Mr. Strack, says the nurse. Right here, says Strack. The nurse hands him a little plastic cup, Strack empties the pills into his left hand, opens his mouth, slams the flat of his hand against it, swallows, gives the little plastic cup, empty, back to the nurse and goes on eating. Mr. Miloslav, says the nurse. Miloslav says, Yeah. The nurse hands him a little plastic cup. Miloslav says, Something wrong here. I only get one. The nurse looks at the compartment with Miloslav's name on it, says, You're right, wait just a moment, takes back the little plastic cup, and Miloslav goes on eating. And Mr. Exter, says the nurse. She hands Exter a little plastic cup, he takes the pill between thumb and forefinger, stuffs it into his mouth, swallows, gives the little plastic cup back and goes on eating.

The nurse leaves. Weyrich, finished eating, stirs his yoghurt, spoons it up, gets to his feet, closes the right hand curtain up to the mid-section of the window, takes off his shoes, opens his pants, takes them off, lays them on his chair, takes off his shirt, hangs it over the back of the chair, lies down on his bed, turns on his side and closes his eyes.

Strack peels his orange, puts the peel on his plate, eats the orange wedge by wedge, picks up Weyrich's cutlery and puts it on his plate, piles his plate on top of Weyrich's plate, stands, takes off his shoes and lies down on his bed.

Miloslav puts his cutlery on Strack's plate, picks up Weyrich's plate and Strack's plate, piles them on top of his own plate, takes his orange and puts it on his bedside table, takes off his shoes and lies down on his bed.

A knock. The nurse comes in and gives Miloslav a little plastic cup with only one pill. Miloslav says, Yeah, that there's more like it, puts the pill on the bedside table, goes into the washroom, fills the little plastic cup with water, comes back and puts the pill in his mouth, swallows, washes it down, gives the little plastic cup back to the nurse, and says, Eh, no problem. The nurse leaves, he lies down on his bed.

Exter peels his orange, puts the peel on his plate, breaks the orange in half, eats the first half, then the second half, puts his cutlery on the plate and piles it top of Weyrich's cutlery, Miloslav's cutlery and Strack's cutlery lying on Strack's plate which is sitting on top of Weyrich's plate which is sitting on top of Miloslav's plate. Weyrich's orange is sitting in the middle of the table. Exter gets up, holds on the edge of the table, goes over to his bed, holds on to the bedrails, goes to up to the door, looks at the city-map, mumbles something and goes out.

A knock, and the taciturn blond in blue smock and white cap comes in, holding a cloth in her right hand. She pushes the dishes to the side of the table, wipes it down, puts the salad bowls inside the yoghurt bowl, puts the pile of bowls on top of the pile of plates, puts Weyrich's dessert spoon in with the knives and forks, picks up the pile of dishes and leaves.

Exter, coming back, leaves the curtain on the left window-section open. He lies down on his bed, turned on his side with his feet hanging over the edge.

Miloslav is lying on his back, hands folded on his chest. He opens his eyes, clears his throat and wiggles his toes.

Strack's head is bent far back over his pillow, his mouth half-open.

Weyrich's left foot is uncovered. His sock has a grey and red pattern.

Exter gets up, mumbles, groans, shifts from one foot to the other, lowers his head, closes his eyes, scratches his head, goes over to the window, comes back to the bed, opens the bedside table drawer, shuts it, sits down at the table, puts his hands on the table, one on top of the other, and lays his head on his hands.

The mid-day nap is over at two o'clock. Miloslav sits up, spreads a newspaper over his knees, takes an apple and a knife out of his bedside table, peels the apple, cuts it into halves, cuts out the core and eats.

Exter raises his head, does a half-turn and looks at Miloslav. Miloslav says, Hope I get out before Christmas. I want to go home.

Far, says Exter.

Miloslav says, Two days' drive. Thousand kilometres a day.

Have to stop someplace overnight, says Exter.

Miloslav says, Yeah. Someplace.

Your family, says Exter, what are they going to

Coming with me, says Miloslav. My wife and my little girl.

Exter says, Two whole days.

My little girl can play, says Miloslav. Or sleep.

Exter says, Be snow on the road.

Not too bad, Miloslav says. The roads are clean. I drive down there twice a year. Always go home for the summer holidays. There's pastures, lakes, sheep and chickens. My little girl can play all she likes. Not like here. Nothing but streets and more streets.

Exter says, Twice a year.

Miloslav says, Been doing it for ten years. My boy's there. With my folks. Couldn't stand it here. Nothing but apartments and streets. He stopped eating, so I took him back. I'm not going to stay here much longer either. The boy's growing up too fast. Maybe only another year. Had enough of this. Built myself a house there, back home.

Exter says, All by yourself.

Miloslav says, Had to hire the electrician and the plumber.

Exter says, Must have saved you a bundle.

Miloslav says, Yeah.

Strack gets up from his bed, straightens his hair, and looks over at Miloslav. Weyrich gets up from his bed, gets dressed, opens the curtain and goes out.

Miloslav says, Been doing piecework for ten years. Built a house, bought a car, furniture, clothes, everything. My wife works too. Lived off her money, bought everything else with mine. Don't have to pay no rent. Got a superintendant's job. My wife does the cleaning, so no rent. I start work at six-thirty in the morning. Been making circuit boards for the last few years. Soldering. Not much to it. Just sitting there the whole time, soldering and keeping your eye on your work. You don't do too bad on piecework. Only you got to be careful. Can't make any mistakes. Got to be fast too. But the money's good. Lot better than back home. When I'm ready to go back I'm buying me a truck. Load the whole thing up, furniture, stuff, wife and kid, and take off. Back home I'm going into the moving business, with my truck. Or drive cab in my car. I'm taking it down first. Just have to see. Main thing's you're healthy. Don't know what happened. Three months ago, suddenly I'm sick. Couldn't get up, couldn't walk. Went to the doctor, asked him, What's the matter with me.

A knock on the door, the nurse sticks her head in and says, They're coming to sing Christmas carols in the front hall. I'll just leave the door open so you can hear.

Exter says, No, don't. Leave it closed.

Strack goes out, shutting the door.

Sound of a choir singing in the hall. Lo, how a Rose e'er blooming.

Miloslav crumples the newspaper around the remains of the apple, goes into the washroom, throws the paper into the wastepaper basket and goes out.

Exter turns and stares out the window.

In the hall there's a trolley with two thermal jugs with taps, one containing a coffee substitute, the other hot water. Beside it, on a second trolley, are cups, saucers, knives, poundcake, butter and jam.

Strack and Weyrich come back to the room. Strack, a cup of coffee and a slice of cake in his hands, sits at the table. Weyrich says, They sang real nice. I know all the songs, used to sing them myself. Before, with my mother. In Dresden.

Exter, against the window pane, says, When was that.

Weyrich says, Last time was when I was seventeen. Twenty years ago. Yeah. Been gone for twenty years now. Haven't sung any of those songs since.

And your mother, says Strack.

Weyrich says, Saw her again two years ago.

Strack, who has eaten the cake and drunk the coffee, goes to the sink, rinses the cup, puts it on his bedside table and remains standing in front of it.

Weyrich says, My folks are coming for Christmas. I want to be out by then. The doctor says I'll make it. Maybe on Tuesday already. Been here long enough this time round.

Strack says, I wish I could say that. But it's completely out of the question. They've had me in here for half a year already.

Half a year's not much, says Weyrich. With me it started when I was seventeen. Twenty years ago. And never stopped.

Strack says, With me it all started in the camp. I had a house of my own over there, you see. I owned it. Built it forty years ago. Right from my front door and into the camp. That's when I knew I didn't have a home anymore. My wife didn't care, she just grabbed everything she could get her hands on. I stopped caring. What for.

Exter says, So why'd you get out.

Strack says, Yeah.

Exter is staring out of the window. At three o'clock the trees in the park in front of the window are filled with the shrill cawing of crows. The birds come flying up and perch on the branches, one after another. Four o'clock, and they shoot up into the sky, black scraps whirled round by the wind. Soon they're all airborne, rising, reeling, diving, climbing in a spiraling swarm, and flying off. The last one leaves the last caw behind. Then all is still.

Weyrich says to Strack, I'm going for cigarettes, want to come. Strack says, You can get them in the machine down by the porter's lodge. Weyrich says, Not Pall Malls. I'm going to the store. Strack says, I'll come, but I'm not going into the store. Reminds me too much of a store I had once. I'm just glad they got a cigarette machine here. Weyrich says, But you got to go inside a store one of these days. What if I never wanted to use a phone again just because I used to work for the phone company.

Weyrich goes to the wardrobe, opens his compartment, takes out a brown coat with a hood, puts the coat on and closes the door. Strack goes to the wardrobe, opens his compartment, takes a scarf out of the sleeve of his brown fur-lined coat, wraps the scarf round his neck, takes out his coat and puts it on, takes out a brown hat and puts it on, and closes the door. Weyrich and Strack leave.

A nurse comes in, hands Exter a magazine and a letter, and says, This was left for you. Exter says, Thanks. The nurse leaves, Exter opens the letter and reads: We know you don't want to see us. We accepted that long ago. But we want to see you.

Exter puts the letter down on the table, opens the magazine whose title is broken by a couple of birds with interlaced wings, seagulls maybe. He reads over the table of contents, turns to page twenty-four, reads an article up to page thirty-three, about a widow and her children, closes the magazine, picks up the letter, reads the telephone number in the letter, puts the letter back on the table, gets up, takes a ballpoint pen out of his bedside table drawer, puts the ballpoint pen down beside the letter, tears off a corner of the envelope, picks up the ballpoint pen, writes the phone number on the corner he tore off the envelope, puts the ballpoint pen down on the table, stuffs the corner of the envelope into the breastpocket of his shirt, gets up, takes a change purse out of his pants pocket, opens it, shuts it, sits down, stuffs the letter back into the envelope, lays the envelope between pages thirty-two and thirty-three of the magazine, puts the magazine on the bedside table, gets up, goes out of the room and down the corridor to the elevator in the hall, presses the button on the wall between the two elevator doors, waits, hears the bell, makes sure the elevator's going down by glancing up at the lights above the elevator door, gets into the elevator, which is empty, presses the G-button and reads two signs: No Smoking, and: By order of the Chief Medical Officer this elevator is out of bounds to unauthorized personnel during meal service, gets out on the ground floor, goes over to the two telephone booths behind the porter's lodge, sees they're occupied, sees three people standing in front of them, a man and two women, and asks if they are also waiting to use the phone. Yes, says one of the women, and other woman and the man nod. Exter looks up at the clock between the two elevators, three minutes go by before a phone is free, the phone booth on the right, which one of the women goes into, leaving three people still waiting to use the phone. Exter looks up at the clock, waits two minutes before the booth on the left is free, which the man goes into, dials, and comes straight out again, saying, Busy, so that the second of the two women can go into the booth, drop her coins in the slot, dial, talk, listen and talk. Four minutes later the woman in the booth on the right comes out again and the man goes in, drops his coins in the slot, waits, shakes his head, hangs up, and comes out saying, Still busy. Exter goes in. The telephone booth smells of perfume, dust, dryness and heat. Leaving the door open, he takes the change purse out of his pants pocket, takes out two ten-pfennig coins, leaves the change purse lying open on the shelf under the telephone, takes the torn-off corner of the envelope with the number written on it out of the breastpocket of his shirt, picks up the receiver with the left hand, the handle is warm, presses the ear-piece to his ear, the ear-piece is warm, drops the ten-pfennig coins into the ten-pfennig slot, looks at the scrap of paper with the phone number on it, looks at the dial, dials three numbers, looks at the phone number, dials four numbers, waits, hears four rings, then a man's voice giving a name. It's Exter, says Exter. It's not true that I don't want to see you. I don't want you to see *me*. The man's voice says something. Exter says, Yeah.

He hangs up, comes out of the phone booth, goes over to the elevator, waits, rides up to the third floor, gets out, walks across the hall and down the corridor, stooped over, head down, hands behind his back, goes back into the room and sits down at the table.

A knock, the door opens and the physical therapist comes in. Now we're just going get a little fresh air, just so you won't forget how to walk, she says to Exter. But it's cold out, so you'll have to bundle up. Exter says, Yeah. He goes over to the wardrobe, opens his compartment, takes out a turtleneck sweater and closes the wardrobe door. I'll just help you, shall I, says the physical therapist. Exter says, Got to do it myself. Good, says the physical therapist. Exter pulls the sweater down over his head, up to the base of the collar, can feel that the collar won't go over his glasses, takes the glasses off under the sweater, gropes for Miloslav's bed, puts the glasses on the bed, pulls the collar down over his head, straightens his hair, puts the glasses on, turns down the collar so he can get at the shirtcollar and straightens the shirtcollar. Now our coat, says the physical therapist. Exter opens his wardrobe compartment, gets out a coat, puts it on and closes the door. Shall we go then, says the physical therapist. She opens the door, Exter goes out, she goes out, shutting the door behind her and saying, Shall we take the elevator or the stairs. Exter says, The elevator. They take the elevator down to the ground floor, get out, walk over to a door which the physical therapist holds open. Exter goes out, the physical therapist goes out. Exter buttons up his coat, turns up the collar, shoves his hands into the pockets, and waits. The physical therapist takes him by the right arm and says, Well, shall we go then. They walk a short distance to some steps leading down from a terrace into a garden, Exter holds onto the railing with his left hand, places his left foot on the top step, places his right foot on the top step beside the left foot, moves his hand along the railing, places his right foot on the second step, places his left foot on the second step beside the right foot, and waits. Everything alright, says the physical therapist. Exter says, Yeah. He looks at the steps and says, Let's keep going, then stops, stands on the path at the foot of the steps, stares down the path and says, But not too far. The physical therapist says, But we haven't even started yet. Barely lifting his left foot, Exter places it the space of a foot in front of his right, drags the right foot after it and places it the space of a foot in front of his left. The physical therapist holds him up. You've got to lift your feet, she says, you can do it. Try. And now we'll just try it a little faster, only a little bit. Exter walks a little faster. You'll be walking again in no time, she says. Exter says, Yeah. Keep your knees straight, she says. Exter says, Yeah.

(1980/1981)

NIGHT OF SECOND AND THIRD OF AUGUST

Fleeing in a group, or on a journey. Arrives at a house abandoned by others who have already fled. A big room with large windows on the second floor. The view from the window: darkness, snow. The radiator under the window, warm, as if he were expected. Amazed, but glad. Has a talk with somebody. The attempt to open the radiator valve wider is successful. The radiator grows warmer. Something, then, can be done. Making preparations for a rest on the flight. There is no furniture, however. Near the house, a pile of cartons, shelves, tools, appliances and utensils. A talk with somebody in the midst of the pile. Various lamps on the ground, some of them burning. A discussion about which of the tools and appliances still work. A few metres away, two men also on the lookout for anything they can use. Far behind the house, a forest that is starting to burn. In the light of the flames, soldiers who have surrounded the forest. Suddenly, tall flames near the pile of boxes, shelves, tools, appliances and utensils. Somebody suggests going back into the house. On the ground floor, in front of an open window. The soldiers are turning away from the burning forest and running towards the house. They are being followed by the fire. Not far from the house two men loom up in the foreground in front of the soldiers. The one, in a long overcoat, a uniform, is helping the other along. They reach the house. The man in the long overcoat, head shaved bare. His face tensed, close. He pushes the other man over the windowsill and climbs into the room. The soldiers have reached the house. They climb in through the window. Whoever was in the room runs out, slipping out of the house on the dark side.

(1981)

MOUNTAIN SKILLS

A man and a woman are driving along a narrow road up a mountain in a light green car. By noon they hope to get a good view of the surrounding mountains, the trees on whose slopes are supposed to be clearly identifiable despite the distance and fog. Having gone high enough, they stop the car on a rocky plateau. To get to the top of the mountain they must negotiate a narrow path between low trees. They can still see the car from around the first bend. And, in a deserted landscape, have to climb an unfamiliar path whose sides are growing with wild plants, both rare and strange. At the top, the heat of the day mingles with the chill mountain air. In their hands, grasses, twigs, as souvenirs. They lay them on the forest floor for a short rest.

On the way back down, which is easy, the man and woman take a long time to study the stones on the path and pick up little peculiarly-shaped ones to take home with them. Before turning the last bend they again catch sight of the light green car on a stone-grey ground against a dark green backdrop of grass and trees. Relieved at the prospect of a quick cool drive into the valley, the man and the woman go up to the car. The man notices it first. The car door is open, the lock destroyed. So is the lock on the other door. The trunk is closed but won't open because the lock has been damaged. Did they leave it open, has the purse with their passports and money been stolen? The car has been ransacked, anything missing? The man and woman just stand there, helpless.

That a young man, evidently a local, steps out from a man-high bush and comes over to them as if he could do something to help, as if he could tell they needed some help, only makes them feel ashamed. With just a hint of irritation, the woman explains away the damage as if it were something that happened every day.

I know a small farm not far from here, the young man says. They'll help you out.

In the car, whose doors are rattling, the drive to the farm is amazingly short. The man and the woman describe the damage to an old woman standing by the fence, but studiously refrain from mentioning the young man who came to their rescue. The old woman goes into a dilapidated, but habitable, house, then comes back and shows them the way to the village with, she says, the only repair shop for miles around.

It's a long way to the repair shop. As the minutes go by, the man is already speaking of the damage as nothing compared to the worst he could imagine. Windows smashed, interior ripped up, tires slashed. Or stolen altogether, the woman adds. The owner of the repair shop is not surprised. He can't replace the locks on the doors but may be able to get the trunk open. It's hard work, without forcing the lock, which resists. Finally the man and the woman have to resign themselves to having it forced open. The contents of the trunk are untouched, their money is still in the purse and the heavy, but unavoidable, damage to the lid of the trunk can now be paid for. But who is going to replace the trunk and the locks on the doors? The owner of the repair shop makes a phone call to the owner of a repair shop in a nearby town, informs him of the damage, tells the man and woman the name of the town and gives them the address of the repair shop.

Next morning, early, the man and woman are on their way.

Now much relieved by thoughts of the anticipated expertise of the already alerted owner of the second repair shop.

All the necessary parts for the light green car are already laid out.

While the car is being worked on the man and woman take a stroll through the town and soon fall in love with it.

The cost of the several hours' labour is considerable, but the man and the woman see only the light green car standing before them good as new. So they always say that the people in the mountains, the village and the town were really awfully helpful.

(1981)

MEN, DULY SWORN

Men, duly sworn, in uniform or in plainclothes, rapid-fire small arms operational, open an apartment door. In the room a man is lying on a cot, wakes up too late, no chance to make a move, which is the way the men want it. As a precaution, however, they order the occupant not to make a move. Be easier if he gets out of bed, he gets out of bed, Hands up, raises his hands, Against the wall, Face to the wall, Much better! says one of the men, the occupant can't see which, Hands glued to the wall. That's more like it.

Men on a search, searching. In the room, in the closet, in the bookshelf, in the desk, under the cot, under the carpet, behind the picture. In the stove in the kitchen, in the cupboard under the sink, in the fridge, in the cupboards, in the garbage pail. In the bathroom cabinet, in the laundry hamper, in the bathroom sink.

In the room, clothes heaped in front of the closet, books in front of the bookshelf, paper in front of the desk; under the carpet, nothing; behind the picture on the wall, a slightly lighter patch of wall. Pots in front of the stove in the kitchen, rags in front of the cupboard under the sink, oats, suger and rice in front of the cupboards, bottles of beer in front of the fridge; beside the garbage pail, garbage. Shaving gear in front of the bathroom cabinet, clothes in front of the laundry hamper, and in the bathroom sink, water.

All done?

Done.

Find anything?

Nope.

Gotta be somebody else.

The occupant, still up against the wall, is told to lower his hands and turn around.

Sorry, the men say. Bye.

2.

At night men, duly sworn and in uniform, rapid-fire small arms operational, take up their positions in front of the doors and windows of a restaurant.

A car has been spotted on the lot beside the restaurant. It's the one. They've got to be sitting in there with all those people in the restaurant. They're young, so it's those young people at the table in the corner there.

After a quick meal the people they've been waiting for come out of one of the doors. The men, who say their piece, weapons in full view, were expecting other faces, different reactions. They take the ones they've got to precinct headquarters in their cars.

Sixty minutes later they know who they are.

Wrong ones, say the men.

3.

Men, duly sworn, in plainclothes, rapid-fire small arms operational, enter a restaurant. They sit at a table next to a table where a man is sitting, who's supposed to be the one they're looking for. They look at him just like men looking at someone sitting at a neighbouring table. They order a coke from the waiter. One of them stands up and goes over to the man sitting at the neighbouring table, weapon in hand. The man, who is supposed to put up his hands, does not put up his hands but reaches into his jacket. That's got to be him. The man standing at the table fires his gun into the man sitting at the table.

That him?

Is now.

(1978)

FÜRCHTEGOTT, HAPPY AT LAST

Fürchtegott, which was his name despite other people's efforts (usually when they were experiencing difficulty breathing) to turn it into something a little more familiar or make it easier to pronounce by mangling it out of all recognition; Fürchtegott took the silver in his right hand and, into his left, counted out a five mark piece, a two mark piece, two one mark pieces and four pennies. At the kiosk in front of the train station, Where I'm going to spend the night, thought Fürchtegott, he bought a curry sausage, sliced, while he still had the money, and, before spearing the first piece with a little plastic fork, asked for a roll, Pretty small roll, Fürchtegott thought, and, taking his time, ate the sausage bit by bit and also the roll. He still had seven mark eighty left but bought neither a beer nor a coke. It was thus a thirsty Fürchtegott who vacated the spot on the left corner of the kiosk and dropped paper plate and plastic fork in a blue plastic bag that smelled of curry sausage, bratwurst, bockwurst, ketchup, mustard, curry, fries, rolls, bread; of paper plates, plastic forks, and cans of beer, Coke and Fanta. He got as far as the entrance to the train station where someone was lying in the doorway fast asleep, a damp spot spreading beneath his pants, Better find a newspaper to lie on, thought Fürchtegott as he just stood there because someone else, with a bottle in his hand, was blocking his way, saying, Have a drink, Great stuff, waving the bottle in his face so Fürchtegott could see the label, vodka, with a picture of a troika and the word Grünberger. Fürchtegott took the bottle, put it to his lips, swallowed, and no, his memory wasn't deceiving him, it really was that cold oily-white taste. He wiped his lips, raised the bottle in acknowledgement of a drink he hadn't seen in a long time, of the town of Grünberg, so near and yet so far, and, somehow or other, of the country which could kindle such a powerful warmth, and gave the bottle back.[1] The other weaved as he took it and said, One of us now, buddy, but Fürchtegott, shunning the brotherly kiss, took a pack of Roth-Händl out of his pocket and offered it to the other man who, however, waved it aside with his left hand, and fumbled around in his own pocket, fishing out a pack of Karo which he brandished over his head. Fürchtegott, already tasting the smooth draw as the pack, held under his nose, gave off an old world aroma, took one and lit it quickly. The other laughed out of comradery, but Fürchtegott didn't like the look of his mouth. What teeth he had were broken.

Fürchtegott blew smoke through his nose, closed his eyes and saw, clearly before him, another train station only a few stops down the line. The building was filled with

---

[1] Grünberg is a town in (former) East Germany, just to the north of – and very near – Berlin. Karo is a brand of East German cigarette; Roth-Händl, a popular brand of West German cigarette. The action here takes place in West Berlin's Bahnhof Zoo railway station, then the meeting place for people who had, in one way or another, gotten out of East Germany.
— *Translator's note*

street smells that rose to his head, gas from two-stro-keengines, clouds of Karo smoke from the door of a tobacconist's, the steam of bockwursts from the air vents of a small snack bar, and, from a store in the corner, even the smell of print from books safeguarding the literary heritage of the nation. Fürchtegott nearly raised his eyes to the bright lettering near the ceiling, which was flashing by with the news, both national and global, apparently oblivious to endless repetition. But the smoke from the Karo, whirled by the breeze, pried open his left eye, and, seeing the other man limping away, he began to think of finding a place to bed down for the night and gave the door to the train station a push.

The curry sausage, the vodka and the Karo had, he thought, been a good omen for the rest of the day, right? Sure enough, he found today's paper in the first trash can he looked, front page torn, sure, but only half-way. Fürchtegott rolled it up and tucked it under his arm. It felt warm. Great, he thought, now for some cigarettes, real cigarettes, Roth-Händl, two-fifty a pack, and some matches, makes it two-eighty. With the paper under his arm Fürchtegott went over to the tobacconist's next to the stairs and bought some. That left him with four-ninety-five. He took a cigarette out of the already open pack in his pocket, ripped the top off all the way and counted six remaining. Somebody with black hands said, Gimme one, and Fürchtegott gave. Smoking his cigarette he walked straight across the hall and down the steps to the washroom. Nice that place in front of rad's free, he thought, but there's room for two, not so cold you have to sleep right in front of it. But he hadn't gone to the washroom to see where he was going to sleep that night. I want to wash my hands before turning in, Fürchtegott thought. The woman, who unlocked the washroom door for him for forty pfennigs, gave the sink a quick wipe and closed the door behind him. That left Fürchtegott with four-fifty-five. There was white soap and paper towels. Wonder what makes me feel like I'm in a washroom riding along on steel wheels, Fürchtegott thought. Nobody's rattling on the door, can't hear any clattering of wheels, either. Maybe it's the light in here, the air, the pale white soap, the grey paper towels? Frchtegott washed his hands and face, dried himself with four paper towels, and combed his hair, which he managed to plaster down in strands. He picked up the paper he'd put down on the floor, tucked it under his left arm and went out. In the big mirror he saw his dirty jacket and dirty pants.

Still time for a little stroll, Fürchtegott thought. The light in the train station was neither bright enough nor dark enough for him. I'll walk up and down in front of the door, he thought, pushed it open and stepped on an empty beer can; and some men, standing around the door, laughed, which gave Fürchtegott a momentary scare, but one of the men, bigger than the rest, who was wearing nothing but an open shirt despite the cold, and whose chest and arms were bright as a shirt from the colourful patterns on his skin, was only being loud for the benefit of the others who were listening to him and laughing. Air's just right for a little walk through the autumn night, Fürchtegott thought, still some light around the silouettes of the houses, but I'm going to freeze without a coat. Better get back inside. Wouldn't mind seeing if there's anybody I know. In the station, Fürchtegott went over to the luggage lockers. A locker with a large suitcase sticking out of it, a man with brown skin sitting on a basket, keeping an eye on the open locker. Fürchtegott remembered a grey pair of pants instead of the blue the man was wearing, a grey jacket instead of one with red and white checks, a jacket with epaulettes and a black belt with a grey buckle, and a grey peaked cap on the man's head. The man was sitting on a suitcase, keeping an eye on a second suitcase standing beside him, the colour of the soldier's skin was white, he was drinking a beer, he looked up at the clock, waited, and watched a traveller take his bag out of one of the lockers, which look just like the lockers in front of me, Fürchtegott thought. Two men and a woman stood beside the man who was keeping an eye on the locker. I'm not going to stand here and let you insult me, the woman said to one of the men. Just come over here if you really want to start something, said one of the men to the woman, and the other said to the first, C'mon, leave her alone, but the woman told him, You just stay out of it.

Now Fürchtegott wanted to feel happy. All I need's somebody to talk to, he thought. So he remembered a name, went to a phone booth, opened the phone book, made a call, and gave his name to the name that answered the phone. That left him with four mark thirty-five. Fürchtegott? said the name. How are you, where are you? — Fine, said Fürchtegott, I'm in town — Come to dinner, we just put it on. — No, said Fürchtegott, but thanks anyway. I just ate. I'm just taking a little walk in the night air and I'm tired. — Where are you living these days. — Right downtown, nice area. — We've got people over, come along, after dinner. —No, really. I see so many people, I just want keep to myself in the evenings, Fürchtegott said. — Suit yourself, said the name on the line. We're having a little party, off on our holidays tomorrow. When are you off? — Oh, said Fürchtegott, Later. Not for a little while yet. — So take care of yourself. And let's hear from you sometime. — For sure, said Fürchtegott. Now he was happy.

He came out of the phone booth, asked a man waiting for the phone what time it was, gave himself another hour and walked around casually. A young man leaning against a pillar told him, under his breath, Get the hell out of here!, but Fürchtegott, looking at him calmly, only shook his head and smiled. He heard a child screaming from over by the ticket counter. Aren't the children in bed yet? he thought. Fürchtegott went around the corner and saw two girls, mothers already, standing together, and two children. The oldest, a girl, was sitting on the floor and was being allowed to stay up and play. The floor was damp from beer cans and covered with cigarette butts. The child, stirring a plastic spoon around inside a plastic container, turned the container upside down and banged out a tune on the bottom of it. When the bough breaks the cradle will fall, Fürchtegott thought, and looked at the younger of the two children sitting up in a tote-bag, but evidently meant to be lying down in it, because one of the mothers, taking a swig of beer, yelled down at it, Get the hell to sleep!, took a drag on her cigarette, pushed the bag up against the wall with her foot, and tossed the second mother a laugh, who also laughed, straightening her long white dress so that the hem reached to her feet. Now Fürchtegott was tired.

But he wanted something to do in case he couldn't get to sleep. I'll just read a bit of the paper, he thought. Thus is my every hour employed in some useful pursuit, and there is no risk of falling short in the account I must one day render of my halcyon days, nor of failing to make the most of my potential.

Fürchtegott left the child that was playing, and the child that was screaming, behind; the mothers didn't even see him. On his way to the stairs down to the washroom he passed a young man, a woman, and two men, but no one paid any attention to anyone else. Only in a city full of people, Fürchtegott thought, can you live in complete anonymity. In the lobby in front of the washroom the space in front of the rad was free. Fürchtegott unfolded the paper, put aside a couple of pages to read, and spread the rest out in front of the rad. He sat down, leaning against the wall beside the rad, and picked up the pages. Men came, going into the toilet, men went, coming out of the toilet. People all around me, Fürchtegott was thinking, yet nobody bothers me. But, he thought, you still live freer in the country, only the pleasures of society are harder to come by. If you want to reach out to an old friend, he could be miles away. You have to learn the art of seeing the best in the people you meet. Comes in handy in the city too, of course, Fürchtegott thought. He looked at the page in front of him. He had trouble with the big letters the newspaper used to advertise itself, and had to spell them out loud to himself. That commerce is everybody's business, he read, is a familiar phrase. A few lines further down he read: We want to be more than a good newspaper. We, he spelled out, also want to serve the society in which we live. But Fürchtegott felt sleep coming on. He laid a firm grip on his money, four mark thirty-five, he mumbled, laid his head in the crook of his left arm and partially covered himself with the paper.

(1981)

EARLY EVENING

Early in the evening of the twenty-eighth of February a young travelling salesman by the name of Saller entered the little waiting room of the train station at Schwäbisch-Hall, a small town not far from Stuttgart.

The air is cold at this time of day, so Saller was glad of the brightness and warmth of the little waiting room. He saw a man lying on the stone floor in front of the stove. Saller pretended not to notice. He looked over the train schedule for the departure time of his train to nearby Stuttgart, looked up at the clock over the door, and threw a quick sideways glance at the man on the floor. Saller noticed that the man was pretending not to notice him.

Saller sat down, keeping an eye on the half-awake man to his left.

There were still seven minutes before the train arrived, eight till it left. Saller estimated it would take two minutes to get to the platform. I've got six minutes, he said.

The man didn't say anything.

Saller saw the man's unkempt hair falling in strands, his dirt-brown face, his thinning beard, his stained jacket with buttons missing, his dark dirt-brown hands, his greasy pants and wet shoes.

Taking a chance, Saller said, It's too cold on the floor.

The man opened his eyes and said, I was going to stand by the stove, but my goddam legs won't hold me up no more. I collapsed. Legs are finished. Sore. Sores big as your hands.

You'd be better off on the bench here, said Saller, pointing to the spot beside him.

Sure, how am I going to get there, said the man.

I could help you, said Saller.

But you can't carry me, said the man.

No, I can't, said Saller.

I managed to scare up a little bread in Schwäbisch-Hall. But not much. People there, real godfearing. Mingy.

Where are you going, said Saller.

Going, said the man. Where do you think. I'm here.

But you can't stay here, said Saller.

How am I suppose to go anywhere? I can't make it alone. And no God and no cop's going to help me. Even if I was screaming for the love of Jesus till I dropped.

You need a doctor, said Saller.

You call it as you see it. Like a prize sap, said the man. Who's going to pay the doctor? You?

No, said Saller. I meant the emergency ward.

Already been, said the man. Quietly told me I was a miserable filthy swine.

You've got to get to a hospital, said Saller.

So where? said the man.

In Stuttgart, said Saller.

Good thinking! said the man. I'll drink to that, worth an Ansbach Uralt at least. I can't even make it as far as your bench, doctor won't come anywhere near me, cops just waiting to kick me out of here, and the Lord God

Almighty couldn't give a damn. Naw, only fairy tales I believe these days are my own.

Saller said nothing.

The train to Stuttgart arrived, Saller got up, said, Good-bye! and went out to the platform.

The man said, He's not going to help me either.

(1985)

SOMETHING FOR EVERYONE, AND NO ONE

Two men, Gaudig and Aberell, were sitting at a table, not saying a word. Because time was hanging heavy on their hands, however, Aberell said, Tell me a story. Gaudig said, I'll tell you the story of the little rooster and the little hen.

Meanwhile Lüning joined them, sat down and said nothing.

Gaudig told Aberell, A little rooster and a little hen were going to Nut Mountain. They made a pact, that whoever found a nut had to share it. Now, the little hen found a great big nut, but didn't say anything because she wanted it all for herself. The nut was so big it stuck in her throat. The little hen was scared she was going to choke, so she screamed, Little rooster, run and get me some water or I'll choke.

Then Lüning lifted his head and said to Gaudig, I don't want to hear that one. Tell me another one.

Gaudig told Lüning, A king had a daughter, beautiful beyond compare, but so haughty and proud, no suitor was good enough for her. She sent them packing one after another and made fun of them to boot. One day the king held a big feast and invited all the eligible men from near and far, who were lined up according to rank and degree. First came the kings, then the dukes, princes, counts, barons, and last, the nobles. Now, the king's daughter was taken down the row, but she had some fault to find with each of them.

Aberell lifted his head and said, So what happened to the little rooster?

Meanwhile Forel joined them, sat down and said nothing.

Gaudig told Aberell, The little rooster ran to the well fast as his legs could carry him, and said, Well, you must give me some water. The little hen is lying on Nut Mountain where she swallowed a great big nut and is going to choke. The well answered, First run to the bride and ask her for some red satin.

Then Forel lifted his head and said to Gaudig, I don't want to hear that one. Tell me another one.

Gaudig told Forel, There was a man who had three sons and nothing but the house he lived in. Each of the sons dearly wanted the house after the father died. But the father loved one son as much as the other, so he didn't know what to do, since he didn't want to sell the house. Finally he had an idea, and told his sons, Go out into the world and learn a trade. The one who is most skillful gets the house.

Aberell lifted his head and said to Gaudig, So what happened to the little rooster?

Meanwhile Mornewey joined them, sat down and said nothing.

Gaudig told Aberell, The litte rooster ran to the bride and said, Bride, you must give me some red satin. I want to give the red satin to the well, the well will give me some water, and I'll give the water to the little hen lying on Nut Mountain where she swallowed a great big nut and is going to choke. The bride answered, First run and get me the little garland that was left hanging on the willow.

Then Mornewey lifted his head and said to Gaudig, I don't want to hear that one. Tell me another one.

Gaudig told Mornewey, There once was a miller who was poor, but he had a beautiful daughter. Now, it so happened that he got to talking with the king, and, in order to make an impression, told him, I have a daughter that can spin straw into gold. The king said to the miller, That is a skill I like very much. If your daughter is so gifted, bring her to the castle tomorrow and I'll put her to the test.

Lüning lifted his head and said to Gaudig, So what happened to the king's daughter?

Gaudig told Lüning, To one she said, What an old soak. To another she said, Long and tall has the faster fall. To a third she said, Fat paunches have lean pates.

Forel lifted his head and said, So what happened to the three sons?

Gaudig told Forel, The three sons were satisfied with their father's plan, and the oldest was going to become a blacksmith, the second a barber, and the third a fencing master. They fixed a day for their return and set out.

Mornewey lifted his head and said to Gaudig, So what happened to the miller's daughter?

Gaudig told Mornewey, The miller's daughter was brought before the the king. He took her to a chamber filled with straw, gave her a spinning wheel, and said, If you have not spun this straw into gold by morning, you must die.

Then Aberell lifted his head and, for the third time, said, So what happened to the little rooster?

Gaudig told Aberell, The little rooster ran to the willow, pulled the little garland down from its branches and took it to the bride, the bride gave him some red satin, he gave the red satin to the well, the well gave him some water, he took the water to the little hen, but when he got there the little hen had choked to death and was lying on the ground, stiff.

Gaudig didn't say any more. He got up from the table and went to the door.

Lüning lifted his head and said, So what happened to the king's daughter?

Forel lifted his head and said, And what happened to the three sons?

Morneway lifted his head and said, And the miller's daughter?

(1981)

TIRED, BUT WIDE-AWAKE

Tired, but wide-awake. About to take a walk. What to wear? Street outside the window, white. From the snow or from the light? Nobody around to ask. Coat, cap, boots. Bag, keys. Down the stairs. Out on the street. Cold snow and hot light. Boots come in handy, coat and cap just more to carry. White leaves on little trees. At the corner, snow hot but light cold. Coat and cap welcome now, boots not. The empty bag, heavy. A sidestreet, rising. Keep going. Step by step in the heat and cold under the weight of the bag. Noise from windows of an empty house. Music, or cries. Shit on white stone slabs. The climb slower. At head-height, sound of the wind, gusting; the leaves on the trees, still. Houses to the left and right, inordinately high. Darkness reflected on sloping roofs. A maze of wires and pipes at the top of the hill. A wide street, no bridge, no supporting cable. Street noise overpowering. Streams of grey cars. Decides to jump down on a roof of a car. Leaping from the roof of one car onto the roof of another, and so on. Boots soaked, coat flapping. Out of breath on the other side of the street. Feeling of hunger and thirst. A door into a low building. A single large space. A voice making announcements over a PA system. From shelf to shelf, from shelf to pile, from pile to pile, from pile to bin, from bin to bin, from bin to pile, from pile to shelf, from shelf to bin, from bin to shelf, shopping cart piled high with cartons, jars, boxes, bottles, cans, bags, tins, tubes, sacks, cart after cart loaded down, shoppers gasping for breath. At the exit, orange-coloured women totaling up each mountainous load with nine quick glances, orange hands reaching for coins and bills. Still in front of the exit, shoppers eating and drinking in the middle of opened sacks, tubes, tins, bags, cans, bottles, cartons, boxes, jars. Still in front of the exit, shoppers stowing mountains of cartons, jars and boxes into every available nook and cranny. At the entrance again, more shoppers, still chewing and swallowing, followed by shoppers who have quickly stowed away bags, tubes and tins. From shelf to shelf, from pile to pile, the low building in circular motion. The motion accelerates. Cartons, jars and boxes falling into shopping carts, shopping carts slipping out of shoppers' hands, shoppers trying to hold onto shelves and bins, orange-coloured women grabbing coins and bills with both arms, plate glass windows falling out of their frames. Sacks, tubes, tins, bags, shelves, shopping carts, shoppers, orange-coloured women, bills and coins in an accelerated flight through the hall and out the windows.

(1981)

STILL SOMETHING, SOMEHOW

He is free, so they say, to use any words he likes. No questions asked. Free from all formal constraints. From censorship. From the rules of the market place. Only the rules of syntax must be observed. Enough of those! Where else would this occasional sense of the bizarre be coming from? (The music, which gives him a jolt, is coming from the first window, right, on the fourth floor of the building at the back, left.)

Only, please, no endless disquisitions on correct spich! There are universities, institutes, experts. Noteworthy also, relevant treatises by the ton, counting only the year 1981.

Begin with what word? Free choice here, too: Before.

Days before. (It was four.) Four days before. The telephone sitting on the chest of drawers in the hall of the apartment, second floor, front block left, rang. It was heard, distinctly, by a man lying on his stomach, eyes closed, on a mattress in the back room. So a man jumped up, did not find the glasses which were lying by his head, and went cautiously but quickly to the phone. I don't believe it, the man said. You, of all people. That is, he mentioned the second reason for his surprise first; the first immediately thereafter: That you'd know where to find me. Uh-huh, said the caller, a woman, lowering her voice on the first syllable and letting it fall on second, but not as low as on the first. What are you up to? she asked. Are you writing? The man remembered it was exactly four days ago. The phone hadn't rung for seventeen days, and then not again for four days.

The one (he or she) who doesn't know who the man (man?) is, where he lives, why he lives where he does, whose house he's living in (why whose), why practically no one ever calls him, why he hardly ever calls anybody, and just happens to hear what he says, may want answers to his (her) questions, such as who he is, where he lives and so on, before perhaps summoning up interest in what else he's got to say. (No).

Yes, the man answered. Sometimes.

He was thinking of a letter he wrote to the medicare authorities five days ago.

Requesting them to cover the remaining cost of having a tooth replaced.

The treatment was long and drawn out. Temporary crowns on filed-down teeth generally lasted a day. Either they slipped off — the man had to suck a crown out of a piece of bread he'd just bitten into, and that in the presence of two diners, a man (woman) and a child, from whom he wanted to hide his embarrassment, being reluctant to reach into his mouth with thumb and forefinger, and afraid they might see the crown in his hand (a lefty) while they were eating, and take it for a tooth (man picks teeth out of his mouth as he eats), and anyway, where would he put it? All he could do was bore into the soggy piece of bread, dig the crown out of the mush and hide it under his tongue. The looks he got from the others, at the wierd contortions on his face! How could he finish his meal.

Or else the temporary crowns broke but stuck, broken, on the filed-down teeth. Sharp, jagged protrusions, like a physical defect.

It occurred to him that he had also signed his name. On a form at the dentist's. (A doctor Helm.)

But he didn't mention the signature on the form, nor the letter to the medicare authorities. Too ashamed because of the caller's concern, and because of her expectations. All the same, she might have been satisfied with a letter and a signature. That was a lot. All things considered. (Pardon?) But the man knew that wouldn't be enough for her. Not even if he assured her he would instantly sit down and write that he had written a letter and signed a form. But then the man would have asked himself, and does ask himself, who's going to be interested in a few lines about teeth?

Which is why he did not answer, Why should I write anything.

The man said, Sometimes I go into the backyard and dump a bag of garbage into the garbage bin. Yesterday an elderly woman was standing at the second floor window at the rear, shouting at me, The one on the end, in the one on the end! There really was still room in the last bin. I knew the old woman. We met last fall by the garbage bins. She was sweeping up leaves that had blown into the yard, and said, Fifty years I've lived here, but I've never seen you before. You're new, aren't you? Yes, I said, I'm new here, in the front. Lots of new people here, she said, mostly young people. They don't know anything about anything. They don't know a thing about the war. How the bombs used to come down. How we used to sit it out in the celler. When I say anything about the war, they say, Yeah, sure thing, war. Nothing to it for them, war. The old woman said, I like to keep the bit of yard in front of my window clean. I want to have something nice to look at, too.

The old woman, the man said, knows the backyard better than I do. I'm learning from her. It is not necessary to describe her. Other people, looking out of their windows, see what I see, too. They look into a window and see a man redecorating a room. On the wall opposite the window he has put up a beach scene with palms high as the ceiling. A girl is sitting in the beach and the ocean is blue. In the yard in front of the window the snow is brown from ashes and black with dirt. Where does the dirt come from? From the street, from the air. It's always been like that, the old woman told me. I answered, But still, it's different. These days anybody who's got a radio knows why it's so hard to breathe. Who owned a radio fifty years ago? You have a radio, don't you. First thing in the morning they tell you there's a bit too much poison in the air. It's a sign of progress, that we're able to be so well-informed. They even tell you what to do about it. Don't heat your stove. Better to sit in the cold when the air is that bad. Don't drive your car. Easy, if you don't have a car. Don't open your window. Even if the air in the room is stale. The air outside is no better. Besides, the room will stay warmer, since there's no heat. And: no smoking. It has its good points. Only they never tell you who's poisoning the air. They say it's regrettable, but necessary so that we can have all the cars, medicine, and laundry detergent we need.

The caller asked, Are you going to write about that?

No, the man replied, I'm just telling you. Who wants to write about it. I don't have the time.

How's that, asked the caller. What are you doing.

Nothing, the man said. I sleep in till noon, wake up in broad daylight and close my eyes. I open them in the half-light of the late afternoon and wait for evening to come on. I try to sleep in the evening, but nights I get up and walk around the room.

The caller said, I don't understand. You have to eat and drink.

The man said, I eat, drink, smoke, stare out the window, go out into the street, buy bread, a pickle, seven tomatoes, and come back. But I do nothing.

That's, I don't know what, said the caller.

I know, said the man.

At least write about not doing anything, said the caller.

(A man picks up a ballpoint pen and paper. He writes— you can look it up— I am doing nothing. As long as he writes he is doing nothing, he is doing something. If he keeps writing, I am doing nothing, he would always be doing something. So he has to keep writing, I am doing nothing. That is how he knows he is doing something. Then he can write: I am doing something. And keep writing: I am doing something. That way, he's doing something. If the caller were to call now and ask, What are you doing ?, he could tell her, I am writing, I am doing something. She could urge him to write about the something he's writing about doing, and he could reply, That's what I *am* doing. Writing, I am doing something, is the something I am doing.)

(The question arises, Who is speaking (writing) here. How can a man, who writes he is doing nothing, be said to be doing anything.) (A detached observer with no hint of favourable bias might add: He doesn't want to live off other people. There have been times when he wouldn't touch a bite unless he paid for it. It did not cost him any great effort of will to refuse it; it stuck in his craw. Symptoms: a groan, a rocking motion of the torso (sideways); gagging; getting up from the table (shuffling his feet); mutters of self-reproach (that is, only partially audible) such as the following: not worth his keep, or (more intense) nothing comes from nothing, etcetera; and (in extreme cases) a silent outburst of tears indicative of sinking under a crushing burden, body accordingly stooped.)

The man said to the caller, One of these days I'll tell you what it's like.

In his mind he was sorting out the details of images for some other time. He imagined the images on a stairs he could go up or down. On the bottom step he kept an image like this: No desire to count for anything anymore, just inert, eyes closed, ears shut, that is, without consciousness of light or sound, unrelated to anything except the passing of time; former thoughts in endless suspension, no feeling of either hunger or thirst—the weaker you get, the easier it is (which is only logical)—day and night emptied out, the distinction blurred, till, just before the final extinction, an animal fear is aroused, inciting the body to go in search of food. Flour licked up from bags that have burst, water greedily swallowed so that it streams down the sides of the face.

On another step, an image like this: The intention to do something, unmistakable, apart from periods (hours) of total exhaustion (numbness ?). Comparisons made— with the desire of the dumb to speak, or of the lame to walk, for example—considered, then rejected as inaccurate. Motion is produced by the intention to get up off the floor; the body raises itself, stands, unsteady, turns to scattered clothes, and remains in the act of reaching for a garment suitable for morning wear.

On the third step, this: Dumping out a garbage bag, buying bread, making a note of the phrase: I am doing nothing.

The caller said, Don't only tell me.

Only you, said the man. You're the only one I'll ever tell that I saw my own death last night. You're dead, said a doctor. Get undressed and report to the autopsy in the basement. I knew that the pathologist was an old friend of mine. Calm and desperate, I went downstairs. My friend let me in without a word, pointing to a table for me to lie down on. I knew this was the last stop. All the same, I was confident we would discuss the results of the autopsy afterwards. Truly a confidence that knows no bounds. My friend smiled; the look on his face, his shoulders, his hands, all said he was sorry for me. The fact that he was going to see all my physical infirmities also made me feel ashamed, even if he was a friend.

But I didn't want to interrupt him till the job was over.

What is happening to you, said the caller.

The man said, A few days before I made an overnight trip to see B. I had heard he was living on a lake so clear you could see the bottom, in a bright, impeccably furnished house kept resolutely clean and tidy, like a model home nobody lives in. What I knew about B. and his wife was that they went around in well-chosen, but not ostentatious, clothes, self-confident and determined to keep up a uniformity of feelings, gestures and speech. I approached the house in the sunshine, from across a meadow. My messy looks and clothes were registered just in time. B.'s wife, in shabby clothes, came running up to me, carrying a table which she set on the grass. Such nice weather, she said, we thought we might as well sit out here. Sure, I said, but kept going towards the house. B. was just coming out. I came to see the lake, I told him. Down to the bottom. He took my arm and led me back to the table on the grass. We stood there. I had to admire the double precautions of my hosts.

The caller said, You should get out more.

I've waded through streets, exhausted, without once looking up, said the man. It was at night. I was afraid of the approaching hour, afraid of the day, and the exhaustion scared me. I was cold, I was hungry, I was thirsty. I stood in doorways to get out of the cold, I smoked cigarettes to forget the hunger and thirst. I should have gone to a pub, got warmed up, had something to eat and drink, but I didn't want to see anybody. Finally I couldn't take another step. I stopped in front of a door that had a card hung up beside it. I opened it and went in. It was practically dark, the only light coming from dim red and blue lamps. I went over to an empty table in the corner, took off my coat, laid it over the back of the chair and sat down. A woman's voice, from in front of the table, said, What'll you have. I looked up and saw that the woman was naked. Sagging breasts, flabby belly, her pubic hair faded and thin. What have you got, I said. The woman said, Whatever you want. I said, I'll have something to eat, and a drink. She said, We don't serve meals here, what'll you have to drink? Beer, I said. Twenty marks, she said. I handed her twenty marks and she put three tickets on the table. The woman brought a bottle of beer, opened it, poured it into a glass and took one of the tickets. I looked up, had a sip, saw the woman go back to the bar, saw a second woman sitting at the bar, naked, and a third woman behind the bar, also naked. I had another sip and lit a cigarette. The woman who had brought me the beer came over to my table, lighter and cigarettes in her right hand, a towel in her left. I'm joining you, she said. She put the lighter and cigarettes on the table and the towel on a chair. How did you find us, she said. Find you? I said. Not much business these days, she said. End of the month. It'll pick up next week. I said, What do you want. Buy me a piccolo, will you? she said. I said, No. She said, I'll give you a blow-job if you want. I said, No. She said, Then I'll jerk you off. I said, No. Oh well, she said, got up, picked up cigarettes, lighter and towel and went away. She sat down beside the woman at the bar, lit up a cigarette and said, You read in the paper where cauliflower's on sale this week? Chicory, too, the other woman said. The first woman said, I wouldn't mind some cauliflower sometime. Think I'll get me one tomorrow.

The other woman said to the woman behind the bar, Turn on the TV.

My field of vision was lit up by the screen. They were running a video of a kitchen. The cook gave an avid laugh, opened his pants and let them fall to his feet. The kitchen maid kneeled in front of him and massaged his balls. The woman who had brought me the first beer came over to my table and said, 'Nother beer? I said, Yes. She brought the second beer and took another ticket. I said, You can turn off the TV. She said, No extra charge.

The woman who brought me the two beers disappeared behind a door. She came back dressed, said goodbye to the other two women at the bar, nodded to the customers and went out. The second woman, who had been sitting naked at the bar, came over to my table. Her breasts were firm, her belly smooth, her pubic hair dark and thick.

She had a candle in her hand, lit it with my lighter, put it in the candleholder and said, 'Nother one. I said, Yes.

The woman brought me my third beer, took the last ticket and said, Anything else? I said, No. I drank half the beer and went to the washroom. A boy was standing in the washroom, smoking, watching me. On the wall over the urinal some one had written: Hot 'n horny boys call, and a phone number. Blacks okay. Written beside it was: Scum like you are disgrace to the white race. And underneath: Nazi swine. Printed above the grafitti was: The emancipation of the workers can only be achieved by the workers themselves. Beside it: Very true. And underneath: Asshole. Go to Poland, why don't you.

I washed my hands. The boy said, Want me to come with you?

I said, No.

I went back to my table, drank a mouthful of beer.

On the TV, a new movie: Lolita in Sweden.

I put on my coat and went to the door. The woman at the bar winked, sang out, Be seein ya!, drank a mouthful of wine and turned her back to me. In the doorway I stepped around some dogshit, frozen, like frozen food guaranteed not to lose its colour or freshness.

The caller said, Go see a friend.

I was thinking of it, the man said, but when the time came I didn't know who it was that was going.

What do you mean, said the caller.

On July the twenty-second, said the man, I woke up to find, lying next to me, myself. My eyes were open and my eyes were closed. There was no doubt about it; but I wanted to know if this was a situation I was in any way familiar with. I remembered sometime or other hearing somebody or other tell me he used to give himself sidelong glances. But he never said anything about parting with himself; he only did it because it gave him pleasure, or to check up on himself. That I was familiar with, but this was something else. Also, I'd often heard it said that somebody was beside himself. I was not beside myself. I just lay there, quietly, waiting. I was trying to find words to describe the difference between me and myself. But soon I became aware that I wasn't going to get hold of me and myself with words. As soon as I tried to grasp the difference between me and myself, the distinction was already blurred, as if in mockery of my efforts. I didn't even know who was trying to find the words, me or myself. So that to speak of myself seemed to be a dubious proposition, yet was at the same time not entirely without some justification. Henceforth I thought of the word "I" for me, and for myself, but couldn't bring myself to decide on two different words. At most it occurred to me to add two little appendages to the word "I" to indicate what was happening, and what would happen, to me, and to myself. I decided, however, to use the word "we" sometimes for both me and myself. Obviously this would only lead to further confusion. Incidentally, it was hard for me at this point to follow my own thinking; I was sleepy, as I've always been in the middle of the night. However, I kept my eyes open and closed. I wanted to get up and I wanted to stay in bed. So I got up and I stayed in bed. *I* called to some one who might have been in the apartment, got an answer, and followed the voice. *I* found no one in any of the rooms, but at least *I* could be happy that some one had answered *me*. With renewed confidence, *I* pursued *my* objective. I was afraid of touching anybody, I was doubled up on the bed in a defensive postion, and *I* was on my feet, looking for somebody in one of the rooms.

The caller said, Call some friends and invite them over.

No, said the man. I never know what to say to them. They look at me as if I were somebody else. Is this really him, or who is it. That just makes me more helpless and hesitant, and then I have nothing to say.

Some time ago, P. called. I'm coming over in an hour, he said. I'm bringing F. with me. We want to see you. Alright, I said, see you then. I got dressed, combed my hair, pushed three chairs up to the table, and waited. I was eaten with anxiety. How was I supposed to sit on a chair. What was I supposed to say. Three times I looked in the mirror to make sure who I was. I sat around the table with P. and F., listening to them talk. P. talked about a novel he'd been working on for three years, which he was trying to sell. The novel was about a summer in California. I was interested in what P. had to say because I can't even imagine what California looks like. I imagined sun, sea, the light-weight clothes the characters would wear. Once I realized that the characters, two men and a woman in light-weight clothes in the sun by the sea, needed a whole summer to find out who belonged to whom, I couldn't understand why the action took place in the summer. So I lost interest in California. P. smoothed down the ends of a white silk scarf he was wearing loosely around his neck.

F. wanted to talk about something else. As I knew, he lived with his wife two days a week, with his girlfriend the other five. I was interested in F.'s words because I wanted to know how he lived with his wife and his girlfriend. It bothers my girlfriend, said F., that I always spend the same two days with my wife, Saturday and Sunday. At first she only wished I'd see my wife on some other day. Now she doesn't want me to see my wife at all. My wife's different, he said. She wants me to spend half the time with her, the other half with my girlfriend.

I kept quiet. I knew that P. and F. were going on as usual. They knew they had to look me up. What was there to say?

What's happened to W., said the caller. Have you seen him.

Yes, said the man. One morning. In a low, wide room. Two or three, probably three, women, plus two men and three children. The women are the first to wake up. Something one of the women says wakes up the men and the children: There's a dead man sitting on the table. The man is grey-haired, frail, with chin on chest, arms folded, feet close together. They all recognize him. Ernst W., says other man. One of the women, the oldest, says, You've got to get him out of here. Who's going to do it, I ask. The woman says, The men can do it. The other man and I go up to the table. Take his arms, I say. We take the dead man off the table; he has stiffened in a sitting position. He's light, to me he seems to weigh no more than his clothes. The other man says, He must have been sitting here for some time. We carry the dead man into the front room but don't know where he's going to sit. Outside it's cold. Be better for him there, says the other man. We carry the dead man outside and put him in front of the door. He lies in a sitting position.

Yes, said the caller. That could be. By the way, the caller said, D. came to see me.

Ah yes, that, said the man.

He'd been to see you, said the caller.

Yes, said the man.

He was trying to get an interview, said the caller.

Yes, said the man. I answered a few questions, then he gave up.

That's what he told me, said the caller.

He did, however, give me the article that came out, said the man. Shall I read it to you?

Yes, said the caller.

Hold on, said the man. I'll get it.

The man put the receiver down on the chest of drawers and went into the back room. The text of the abortive interview lay under a pile of unanswered letters.

You still there? said the man.

Yes, said the caller.

Here's what it says, said the man.

Answer: Do you see this writing pad? That's chapter twelve of a novel. Not one word of it remains. Every word crossed out, then replaced. The revisions are also rejected. So are the revisions of the revisions. When the page is full it is destroyed. Torn up. We thus have a notebook without any pages.

Question: How long have you been working on your novel.

Answer: Four years. I'll be finishing it this year. It takes up sixteen empty notebooks.

Question: What is the theme of the novel.

Answer: The spoken word. Something is said; but a word, once spoken, vanishes. There is really only one way to describe the spoken word: the vanished word. Therefore, the record of the spoken word must also vanish.

Question: The words you are speaking now are not going to vanish.

Answer: That's what's wrong with this interview.

Question: Couldn't you let a page of your novel out of your hands before you tear it up?

Answer: I never let unfinished work out of my hands.

Question: It wasn't easy to find you. Why are you living in isolation.

Answer: I'm not. I go to the store every day to buy a paper. Twice a week I go to the supermarket and buy groceries; for example, bread, tea, tobacco.

Question: Do you have any contact with the people in your neighbourhood?

Answer: I run into the superintendant on the stairs. We say hello and talk about the building. I meet an elderly woman on the stairs. We say hello and talk about aging. I see someone at a window and I nod to them.

Question: Is that the extent of your social life?

Answer: Yes.

Question: Do you have any contact with other writers?

Answer: Rarely.

Question: With whom?

Answer: With a colleague in the city here. It's too far to walk, so I go by subway. But most unwillingly, because it's underground.

Question: No contact with any other writers?

Answer: Oh yes. Recently, when I was visiting the one who lives in the city here, the phone rang. My colleague told the caller that I'd just dropped in for a visit. The caller, so my colleague told me, said, Oh, so he's still alive?

Question: Where do you get experiences to write about then.

Answer: I remember them. Mind you, I must admit that some of my memories are missing. For example, I don't remember ever having killed anyone. When I think about it, the question arises: Have I really never killed anyone or is my memory failing.

Question: But the memory presupposes the experience. How can you remember something you've never experienced.

Answer: As I said.

Question: Would you care to give an example?

Answer: I remember being under a high dome, swinging from a trapeze. The swinging gave me great pleasure, but also inspired mortal fear. Curious as to the possible height of the pleasure, I swung higher. My hands couldn't take the weight. But I couldn't stop feeling pleasure.

Question: How does it end.

Answer: I don't remember.

Question: A lot of people worry about a possible outbreak of war. What can a writer do to work for peace?

Answer: Whose peace do you mean?

Question: World peace.

Answer: Oh well, you know.

The caller said, Go on.

The man said, The interview ends here.

Wouldn't you know, said the caller.

I'm tired, said the man.

Keep your wits about you, said the caller.

Sure, said the man.

He hung up. He stood in front of the phone, helpless. Somehow, still something left to say, he said. But the need (strong/ pressing/ acute/ or lacking an appropriate adjective) to say something without knowing what (and: had it been conscious he wouldn't have found a word for it) was exhausted with the expression of the need. Although he knew that whatever it was, was something more than the need to express it.

(1982)

INTENSIVE CARE

I thank all those who told.

Elizabeth Kramer says, All I know is, he didn't want to be a shopkeeper, but they made him go to business college anyway. He was so, so withdrawn, keeping to himself. A loner, that's what he was.

Our house wasn't much of a home. Our father wasn't much of a father, didn't understand his children at all. Besides, he drank. But he was a hard worker and did very well for himself. When I think he lost three hundred twenty thousand marks in the currency reform.

Had a car in nineteen-eleven already. Took me to my christening in a car, in nineteen-eleven. Mother told me, When the christening was over and we were ready to go home, the car wouldn't start. We all had to go to a pub in the little hotel next to the church, in Kirchnitz. Nineteen-eleven, and he had a car already. So you could say he was a man of ambition. Only the alcohol kept getting in the way. His parents, they didn't drink. Grandfather Ruttig, I can still remember him, and grandmother. Came from a poor family, our father. Just wanted to do a little better.

Had trouble making friends, though. Except when he was drunk. Not a happy man, our father. In Oberlangenreuth he was always Mr. Ruttig. Nobody ever called him Paul. Never had any friends in the village, either. Oh yeah, they'd call him Paul, the farmers, when they were drunk. When he'd pile them into his car at five o'clock in the morning and drive to the next pub that was still open, in some other village, like Bertoldsgrün or Irnfriedsgrün. When he'd head out along Kirchnitz street, with them nearly flying through the roof of the car. Some street that was, full of runnels, for the water to run off. Early the next morning, eight o'clock, their wives'd be over at our place. Say, Mrs. Ruttig, your husband come home yet? So where is he then. No sign of our men, doesn't look like they're ever coming home, what'd he do with them.

Fritz was a quiet boy, kept to himself a lot. Sure liked to play the piano, though. He could do it all by himself, nobody ever taught him. That was his one joy. I was supposed to learn to play the piano, don't have musical bone in my body. I'd never've been able to play from memory. But Fritz was musical. Instead of letting the boy learn the piano, making him do that.

He was born in nineteen-o-five. Trudi was born the year before. Erwin before that, who died as a child. Before Erwin there was Erna. Before Erna, Hilda, nineteen-hundred. And Alfred, the oldest, in eighteen-ninety-five. After Fritz there was Gottfried. After Gottfried, Karla and Ernst, the twins, nineteen-o-nine. Ernst died at birth. I came along in nineteen-eleven. And Werner in nineteen-sixteen. He was the last.

Father was always picking on Fritz. Couldn't stand him. Always grousing at him. Fritz never said anything, but he was often very unhappy. That I know. Yes, very unhappy, often. Because he was always alone. Because he always kept to himself. What could he do.

Fritz went to business college like father wanted. Other boys from our village too, the baker's boy and the neighbour's boy, all took the train into the city. Fritz never sat with them. Used to sit by himself. Maybe he never had a girl either.

Werner, when he was old enough, he went to school in Weissberg, from twenty-seven to thirty-two, till he got his junior matriculation. Father sent him to boarding school in Weissberg. Why, I don't know. Maybe because Werner was a bit small and frail, being the last, you know, so he wouldn't have to make the long trip from Oberlangenreuth into the city every day. And Alfred, the oldest, he'd been to school in Weissberg too. In the seminary.

Fritz used to ride a motorbike. Oh yes, he had a motorbike. Father bought it specially for him, used to deliver wool samples with it, for father. One day he picked Werner up in Weissberg. In Thomberg this big rooster ran into the motorbike. So him and Werner got thrown from the bike. Weren't hurt, though. Only his lovely leather jacket got torn. They called home and father went to pick them up in the car. Fritz couldn't ride the motorbike home. He was in shock. Not hurt. Or maybe he was, I don't know. Anyway, that's what did it. It was a big shock for him. He was the serious type. Never did anything stupid.

He studied hard, when he was in business college.

George Kramer says, Karla says, Fritz got a job in Bittelbach after he finished school, in a canning factory that had a store attached. Father took him out of there. Said, What's that got to do with textiles.

Elizabeth Kramer says, Had to work in father's shop after that. Just didn't like it very much. He didn't like father very much either. Used to upset him terribly, the fact that father drank.

Thea Langner says, Werner says, Father wanted one of his sons to take over the business. But Alfred, the oldest, became a teacher. Gottfried became a farm manager; he was killed in an accident, by the drive-belts on the threshing machine. Fritz was next in line. He was brimming with life, played piano divinely. Fritz wanted to be a musician. Father wouldn't hear of it. He forced him to go to business college. Fritz often played for the dances at the school. Then he was suddenly so different. He was unlucky in love too.

Elizabeth Kramer says, He was bad, father, real bad. Brutal. If mother ever said anything about him being drunk, he'd lay into her. Once, in the kitchen, she was making preserves when he threw her against the stove.

But mother wasn't too smart either. Usually she was quiet and never said much. But times like that, when father was drunk, she always had something to say. One day she just had to go and say something again. Father lost control. Completely. Eyes popping out. Hollering. Like a madman. So we got out of there, up to the top of the attic and shut the trapdoor. Mother, all of us, anybody who was around. Because we were afraid of him, because we thought he was going to do something to us.

Oh, he was already drinking before. At first our parents lived with a Swabian in Oberlangenreuth, in the upper village, practically in Hartungsgrün. Father only built our house later, in nineteen-o-two or three, I think. Trudi was born in the house in nineteen-o-four. Mother told us she used to go into the village, nights, to bring father home from the pub. Feustel's. She was afraid father might fall dead-drunk into the mill-race.

Next door to us lived the Teicherts. I went to school with Elli Teichert. Mrs. Teichert said she was sorry for mother. Mrs. Teichert used to do the cleaning and washing for mother, even though she had four children of her own. She said she was sorry for mother because father drank.

Back when we were living in our house, our parents' house, and I was old enough to understand a few things, I noticed that father was perfectly normal when he was in the shop. The shop was in the house. Used to get up early in the morning, he was vain, and he was clean, washed himself every morning, stripped to the waist. We didn't even have a bathtub. Washed himself in the kitchen every day, put on his best clothes and went into the shop. We always had coffee in the kitchen, early. Then he'd go to work.

But come five o'clock in the afternoon, he'd put on a coat, take his walking stick, and off he'd go. Made as if he was going for a walk, and always ended up in some pub somewhere, Bertoldsgrn or Infriedsgrn, that's how far he'd go. Wouldn't come back either. He used to go to Feustel's a lot too. Hartungsgrün had a couple of pubs, used to go there too. A regular. Always came home tipsy. Always. Even on weekdays. Sometimes he wasn't too drunk, sometimes a lot. And if mother ever said anything. I never loved my father. Not even a little bit. But I couldn't understand my mother either. I used to think, That she puts up with it. And I thought, I'd take my children and get out of there. But you couldn't do that. Not as if she had any education or training. So what was she supposed to do. That mother just put up with it. She was anyway the patient type. Since then I hate everybody who drinks. I always had such a hate on drunks that I hate anybody who drinks.

When that thing started with Fritz, Fritz stopped shaving, didn't wash himself properly anymore, stopped caring about how he was dressed, just went out and didn't come home all day. Wandered all over the fields, alone. I never really noticed because he was always a quiet, lonely type. He was very good to mother. He loved mother very much.

When Hilda got married, nineteen-twenty-eight, Fritz was already sick. Hilda had a boyfriend who was an engineer, an educated type. Hilda was educated too. Our Hilda, she educated herself. To start with, she was musical, could sing beautifully and play the piano. She sang like a meadowlark and she'd play and she'd play and she'd play. And then she also read a lot of books.

She'd been going with the engineer for a long time, in Dresden. She was head over heels in love with him.

He came to see her one time. So there he was at our door. A distinguished man, an engineer, a civil engineer. He built bridges. After he'd been at our place and met Fritz, he broke off with Hilda. That's what she said, It was because of Fritz. Probably didn't want to marry into a family with something like that running rampant. That really finished Hilda. She married Heintze out of sheer desperation. They weren't even suited to each other.

Fiebig was the engineer's name, Willi Fiebig. He was always giving Hilda books. The house was full of books we got from him: For my beloved Hilda, your Willi. He was the big love of her life.

My Hans, he still met Fritz too, in nineteen-thirty. He could have dumped me too. But he stuck by me.

Fritz, he just kept running away, often didn't come home. Where he went, I don't know.

George Kramer says, Karla says, When he grew restless or got frightened, he'd go into the woods.

Elizabeth Kramer says, Father would have a fit. But.

George Kramer says, Karla says, Father should have been a little more loving towards Fritz.

Elizabeth Kramer says, Once he took off on a train. No money, nothing. In December, twenty-eight. Got as far as Munich. Father told the police to haul him off to Bethel. Didn't even want him back.

He wrote to Bethel: ... concerning my twenty-three year old son, Fritz, who has gone to business college but has never been able to hold down the various jobs he's had due to his obstinacy and inability to conform, so that he has been unemployed for four years now, and sitting around the house while I support him on the meagre income from my shop.

For a year now he has been under the delusion that he does not have to work anymore, smokes like a chimney, especially likes to ride around in rented cars, and runs up debts wherever anybody will lend him any money.

My small business and my large family (eight children) do not permit me to discharge the financial responsibilities which the boy lays on my shoulders, and so I have for some time now withdrawn my financial support. He has been away from home since the fourth of this month, and we have had no word of him until now, when early this morning an inquiry from Munich police headquarters arrived in the mayor's office here, wanting particulars about my son. I presume he has been picked up as a vagrant in Munich, and have arranged for him to be transferred to your institution, especially since I have already had urgent medical advice to have him put in a mental home.

There is no doubt the boy is mentally ill but I leave it to you to decide what ward you want to admit him to.

I am confident that, with suitable treatment, you will be able to straighten the boy out.

My family and I live in modest circumstances, so there is no need for his institutional care to be any different.

Please send all charges to me, yours faithfully, Paul Ruttig.

Elizabeth Kramer says, But they wouldn't take him. He had to come home again.

You should have seen him. Dirty, unshaven, thin, sad.

Fritz had two different eyes, one light, one dark. One grey, one brown. Mother had brown eyes. But what colour father's eyes were, I don't know. We were all scared of father.

I got myself a page-boy cut, when I was seventeen. I was scared to go home. I bought myself a hat and sat down to supper, wearing the hat. So he said, You gone crazy or something? Sitting at the table and eating with a hat on? Take that hat off!

Then he saw it. But he didn't do anything. Karla said, You always were your father's favourite.

He sould have sent me to school. I would've learned something, I wanted to. Sent all the boys, they weren't even interested, but never let me go.

He sent me to business college from nineteen-twenty-six to nineteen-twenty-eight. Cost a lot. He had to pay for the whole thing himself. But I wasn't interested. Bookkeeping. I didn't want anything to do with business.

I met Hans at the beginning of nineteen-thirty, January first, thirty. In Helleneck. I was eighteen, he was twenty-two. My oldest brother, Alfred, he said to me, Your friend's a little Kike, isn't he. I didn't even know what that was. So I said, What on earth's that. You know, a Jew, he said. Hans had given me a beautiful photo and I used to show it around proudly at home. We got engaged in October, thirty.

That's when Fritz ended up in Rodewisch. In the looney-bin.

Father said, He's crazy.

Probably arranged by some doctor. In Bittelbach. Doctor Unglaub.

Schizophrenia, they said. That's what the doctors told our parents. Schizophrenia.

Must have run in the family. After all, Trudi was sick too. And her two girls. Monica and Margot. Their father, Harold Heinz, he drank like a fish. And then our blood on top of it, what a mix. Well, no wonder.

Karla was sick too. I wasn't. Alfred wasn't. Hilda wasn't. Erna wasn't. Werner wasn't. Gottfried used to do some pretty stupid things. Well, stupid. He was the way boys are. He was supposed to go to high school, didn't interest him at all, he liked to hang out with the farmers.

We often went to visit Fritz in Rodewisch. Drove there in the car. Father and mother always, me sometimes, sometimes Trudi. One of the brothers or sisters always went along.

A terrible place. An old lunatic asylum. Huge windows, with bars. A large waiting room. They'd bring Fritz out. Benches in the waiting room, windows there barred too.

So we'd sit there with him. We'd give him all the stuff we brought along with us. But we weren't allowed in where he lived. I never did see it.

Fritz got worse in Rodewisch. That's where he reallly took ill. He wasn't so bad before. That's where it really happened.

Often he didn't even know we were there. Mother always cried, gave him something to eat, or whatever. And him, everything about him so mechanical. Wasn't really aware of us.

George Kramer says, Karla says, I went with mother to see Fritz. The nurse said, Just a moment, I'll get your son. He came, mother took him over to the window. Fritz, he says, You come from Denmark, right, mom.

That really hurt.

Vera Wolff says, We often went to visit Uncle Fritz in Rodewisch, my parents and me. He was always peaceful and friendly.

Elizabeth Kramer says, Father, he didn't do anything. Did he talk to Fritz. Not on your life.

My father wasn't the type to talk to doctors. He wasn't like that. First of all, there was this notion, you got a crazy son, it's a disgrace. And then my father wasn't the kind of person who'd even be interested, I mean in a human way. He never spoke with the doctors.

Herta Ruttig says, He was a harsh man. Not at all a good man. I was always afraid of him, my father-in-law.

His wife, what did she ever get out of life? Eleven children in twenty-one years. And a man like that.

Vera Wolff says, I was always afraid of grandfather. My father taught me not to speak in front of grandfather unless I was spoken to. I was never spoken to. My father was afraid of him too. His own father.

Elizabeth Kramer says, We got married in April, thirty-one, Hans and me. In September George came along.

I don't even remember my wedding. All I know is I cried the whole day. And I know why. I didn't want to get married. I was miserable because I had to get married. I never wanted to get married, ever, and there comes Hans and saddles me with a kid. I never even wanted to sleep with him. Not that I got much out of it. First time in bed with a man, and a kid already.

Hans, he said, Don't be unhappy. I'll fix everything.

That's where Gerda, Hans' sister, was smarter. She went to this SS school for brides, where they got cleared up about the facts of life. She was smarter than me, she never had to get married. Boy, was I dumb.

I didn't want to get married. I wanted to study and get out in the world.

Later, after we had a few kids already, Hans went to Rodewisch. Wanted to find out all about it. After we already had children, that's when he told me, You know, we shouldn't have had any children. Because of Fritz. You never know if it's going to show up again. Or in the grandchildren. He was scared.

Fritz was in the asylum till he died. Till they murdered him. That was nineteen-forty, when they did it.

I was visiting mother and father when the letter came, that Fritz died from a lung heamorrage, that he'd already been cremated and they were sending us the urn.

The letter, we were in the living room when we read it, father, mother, me too.

Thea Langner says, Werner says, I read the letter too. It said: Died of lung-haemorrage.

George Kramer says, Karla says, Passed away from a haemorrage of the lungs. Said so.

We had to believe it.

Elizabeth Kramer says, Mother, she couldn't believe it. She didn't even know Fritz wasn't in Rodewisch anymore, mother and father never knew a thing about it.

The letter came from somewhere else completely.

They must have killed Fritz shortly after they evacuated him, or my parents would have known he wasn't in Rodewisch anymore. It's not as if they never went to see him.

They got rid of the patients, and when they were dead the notification would come from such-and-such a place.

The letter came from Linz, on the Danube.

My parents had to face the fact that Fritz was already cremated and they were getting the urn.

Mother, she said, So far from home, so very far.

It was a mystery. Fritz, suddenly supposed to have died in Linz.

This small urn arrived, such a little thing. Father and mother could hold it in their hands.

Hans didn't know what happened either.

Nobody had a clue. Only guesses. Thought maybe Rodewisch was needed for the soldiers. Maybe it was turned into a military hospital.

Untergöltzsch Mental Hospital, it was called. Untergöltzsch Mental Hospital.

Thea Langner says, I heard Untergöltzsch was used as a military hospital during the war. Obergöltzsch Home for the Aged was too, I heard.

Ernst Klee says, We must begin with the assumption that Fritz Ruttig was murdered at Hartheim, which may be inferred from both the alleged death certificate and the fact that the notification came from Linz. There are no surviving records from Hartheim. There was a mass transportation from Rodewisch in particular, because the resident doctor there—doctor also in the sense of Nazi war-criminal—supplied false diagnoses.

In a report of thirty-first October nineteen-forty-two on his inspection of the medical records of the Rodewisch Home for the Aged, Doctor Wischer, an expert from the Berlin Centre for Euthanasia and Director of the so-called Waldheim Transit Clinic in Saxony, states: District Auerbach Home for the Aged (Vogtl.); Postal Station Rodewisch (Vogtl.); (formerly Obergöltzsch District Home for the Aged).

Report:

The actual home with ca. 200 beds has been entirely requisitioned by the Wehrmacht for tubercular soldiers. Two units at the facility at Untergöltzsch have therefore been put at the disposal of the home for the aged, 107 patients having been housed to date.

The home belongs to the District of Auerbach and is at this time under the direction of Inspector Kirchhoff.

Auerbach District Chief Administrator— Dr. Becker— had previously rid the home of all feeble-minded and mentally ill patients, and in future only genuine cases of old age will be admitted. For this reason there were no new registration forms to complete. One is left with the impression of quite a competent and sensible administration.

Worth noting are photostats of a large number of deliberately false diagnoses, prepared in his time by Dr. Epperlein, then doctor under contract to the home. Dr. E. is also the mayor of Rodewisch (in an acting capacity) as well as a practising physician, and has been decorated with the Medal of Honour. The diagnoses are all slanted towards a negative evaluation; thus the slightly feeble-minded are diagnosed as "idiots", etc. Rodewisch, 31.10.42, signed, Dr. Wischer.

Ernst Klee says, Yet we cannot exclude the possibility that the certificate of death was merely issued at Hartheim, while Fritz Ruttig was killed in some other facility closer to Rodewisch.

Thea Langner says, Patients from the Untergöltzsch Mental Hospital were evacuated, also the mentally ill from the Obergöltzsch Home for the Aged. The remaining patients from the Home for the Aged were housed in two buildings at the Untergöltzsch Mental Hospital. Both Home for the Aged and Mental Hospital were used as military reserve hospitals. Ernst Klee says, Death by asphyxiation, to free up beds for the military.

Elizabeth Kramer says, What they were doing to the insane, we didn't know till, oh, we really didn't know anything about it in nineteen-forty. Who knew anything about it back then, forty years ago. That's how long Fritz has been dead.

Vera Wolff says, Right away my father said, They've murdered Fritz. Fritz was in good physical health.

Vera Wolff says, That put a damper on grandfather's enthusiasm for the Nazis. Grandfather was a Nazi through and through. He didn't need a uniform or a Party badge. He contributed large sums to the Nazis in Oberlangenreuth. But he stopped after that. He was more angry than sorry over that business with Fritz. Now he's got up a good hate for the Nazis, my father told me.

Elizabeth Kramer says, Actually father wasn't a Nazi. Always used to get the Social Democratic paper, before. It was Hans made him a Nazi. Hans told father he should join the Party, so he did.

In Helleneck Hans set up an Anti-Department-and Co-op Store Action Group[1], and led it till the summer of thirty-three, when we moved to Oberlangenreuth. In Helleneck he'd taken over a small drugstore, in the spring of twenty-nine, for his father. His father, Oswald Kramer, owned a big drug and grocery chain, with a distillery and a coffee factory.

Hans also joined the Party in Helleneck. End of thirty-one. Right away in Oberlangenreuth he was active in the Party again. He was in charge of the local Party office, then head of the local Party branch. Hans could really convince people. So could my father.

---

[1]Nazi-inspired initiatives on the part of small business, which used agitation against large department store chains as a pretext for anti-semetic attacks.
—*Tanslator's note.*

But at first his customers, the local businessmen from Bittelbach, always used to say to him, Come on now, Mr. Kramer, admit it, You're really a Yid, aren't you? So he went and plastered his hair down with water.

Vera's father, our Alfred, he wasn't for the Nazis. He was against the Nazis. But he joined the Party too.

Thea Langner says, Werner says, Fritz was taken to Rodewisch in nineteen-thirty. Nineteen-forty he was evacuated from Rodewisch to Zschadrass near Leipzig, and from Zschadrass to Hartheim near Linz. The announcement of his death came the same year. Nineteen-forty, from Hartheim. That I know. I saw the letter myself.

Thea Langner says, Werner had to go and fight in the Polish campaign. He got case of ulcers that needed operating on. That's why he can remember the date exactly. That business with Fritz happened right after. Nineteen-forty.

I've heard that men on the Polish campaign saw sick people and Jews being murdered. Maybe Werner saw it, so he knew what happened to his brother. Because he was convinced, back then already he says, that it was euthanasia. Murder.

Thea Langner says, When I heard Werner mention Zschadrass, it reminded me of a Zschadrass Sanitorium Seventy-Fifth Anniversary volume I had once. I had to spend a whole day looking for it, but I found it. Underneath my road maps and city guides. In Commemoration of the Seventy-Fifth Anniversary of Zschadrass Sanitorium, Eighteen-Ninety-Four to Nineteen-Sixty-Nine. In there it says who the medical director was from nineteen-twenty-nine to nineteen-forty-five. Doctor Liebers. A psychiatrist.

There's also something about the history of the place. About the Nazi era it only says: Shameful and disgusting procedures for euthanasia and sterilization were implemented after 1933 and 1939. The veil obscuring these horrible events was lifted only many years later.

The introduction begins with: The staff of Zschadrass Sanitorium proudly look back on its first three-quarter century of existence. Its eventful history shows how the aims of the institution have changed along with the evolution of medicine over the coarse of time.

Thea Langner says, I know few doctors interested in the subject of euthanasia. When I was studying medicine in the fifties it was never mentioned. At any rate, I don't remember that it ever was. Interest in the subject was sparked only later, in intensive therapy research, when the issue of limits to resuscitation came up.

Thea Langner says, After the war, Zschadrass Sanitorium became a psychiatric clinic again. And a TB-clinic and a lung-clinic. Like before, from fourteen to twenty-four.

Ursula Plog says, In the past, people with contagious diseases and mental problems were housed in remote clinics, people with tuberculosis and the mentally ill, for example.

Ursula Plog says, As children we had to go to South Heppenheim to be x-rayed. South Heppenheim had a psychiatric clinic that had been a TB-clinic at one time. The x-ray machines, the ones they were going to use on us, were still there from before. But we knew, we used to say, it was an insane asylum. There was a rumour, a sense of death about it. We were all scared of these x-ray machines. You had go into this little booth all alone, and then it suddenly got smaller. The gassing, that they did it in the bigger rooms, I only heard about later. For me, gassing was always associated with the little x-ray booth. For me it was scary, having to go in there for an x-ray. It spelled danger.

Thea Langner says, Today I got hold of the file card on Fritz. They found it in the archives in the basement the Untergöltzsch clinic in Rodewisch. It wasn't in the usual place, but in a special box. But they didn't find the medical file. It must have been sent on to Zschadrass or even further. Under Admittance and Discharge on line three there's a big W in red pencil. What does that mean? Is that Doctor Gerhard Wischer's initial, the euthanasia expert who made the so-called inspection of Rodewisch?

The card has the following entries: Ruttig, Fritz. File No: I2392. Patient No: 110/30. Clothing allowance No: 59. Registration No. is crossed out. Written in is: low rate. Birthday: 16.11.1905. Place of Birth: Oberlangenreuth. Reg. No: 57, Oberlangenreuth Registry Office, District Plauen. Profession: shop assistant. Religion: Evangelical Lutheran. Social Assistance Office: /. Citizenship: German. Marital Status: single. Children: /. Admitted 22 May 1930. Discharged 30 July 1940. Referral from: Oberlangenreuth. Last Place of Residence: Oberlangenreuth. Charge to: Plauen District Administration, now father. Discharged to: Zschadrass. Parents: Paul R., merchant. Mother: Martha, née Drfel, both: Oberlangenreuth 20D, Bittelbach. Other Relations: 7 brothers and sisters.

Hans Marsalek says, When Hitler introduced his euthanasia policy at the end of October nineteen-thirty-three, retroactive to first of September nineteen-thirty-three, a total of six clandestine facilities for the killing of the mentally ill were established within the borders of the Reich. These euthanasia clinics were located in Brandenburg near Berlin, in Hadamar near Frankfurt am Main, in Sonnenstein near Dresden, in Grafeneck near Stuttgart, in Bernberg near Naumberg, and in Hartheim. At Castle Hartheim there was a gas chamber disguised as a bathroom, a crematorium and a bone-mill. The victims were killed with cyanide gas.

Hartheim's first victims were child patients already evacuated from the castle in the summer of nineteen-thirty-nine and transferred to a so-called transit facility. The Hartheim Euthanasia Clinic was administered by Doctor Rudolf Lonauer, a junior doctor from Linz, and his deputy, Doctor George Renno, from Germany. Both were fanatical Nazis. The temporary head of administration was Franz Paul Stangl, a former detective of police and later commandant at Treblinka death camp. The clinic employed eighty-two people, almost without exception all members of the Nazi Party. They received special pay and had to sign an oath of secrecy. Doctor Lonauer comitted suicide in May nineteen-forty-five. Doctor Renno was acquitted by a court in the Federal Republic of Germany. Stangl was arrested in South America in nineteen-seventy-six, extradited to the Federal Republic and sentenced to life imprisonment. He died in prison.

Ernst Klee says, We know relatively little about Doctor Lonauer. We know rather more about Doctor George Renno, who, after the war, managed to obtain a fake driver's licence in the name of Doctor Reinig and work as a relief doctor under the assumed name. Allegedly, the regional college of physicians did not ask to see his licence.

As Doctor Reinig, then, he thereupon becomes a research scientist for one of the big drug companies. Nor does the company bat an eye, when, in nineteen-fifty-five, its researcher, Doctor Reinig, turns into Doctor Renno and produces a licence in that name.

Hans Marsalek says, Under the provisions of the euthanasia policy, the mentally ill were subsequently evacuated from the various sanitoria and nursing homes. They were then transported to the death clinics in batches. Besides the mentally ill, inmates from Mauthausen-Gusen and Dachau concentration camps, who were unfit to work, were also sent to the gas chambers at Hartheim. In his September nineteen-forty-five deposition before the Linz Criminal Investigation Department, a witness, Vincent Nohel, estimated the total killed at Hartheim to be in the neighbourhood of thirty thousand. The total of thirty thousand dead may be taken as an approximate figure.

Written communications, from the time of the victim's selection in the original institution to his death, followed a standard pattern throughout the Reich. The last notification of change in the patient's condition ordinarily announced the news of his passing. Diagnosis of death almost always followed a uniform pattern, and relatives were notified according to an adaptable formula. The bogus cause of death was followed by some fiction about the necessity of immediate cremation of the remains, the death clinic generally passing itself off as a centre for disease control. The notification closed with instructions on the delivery of the urn.

An employee of the Upper Austrian Co-operative Welfare Society employed at Castle Hartheim from nineteen-thirty-four to nineteen-thirty-eight, Sister Felicitas, gave the following report on the activities there: My brother Michael, who lived at home in Alkoven at the time, told me in strict confidence that former patients were being burned. He made me swear not to say anything because the people of Hartheim and vicinity had been threatened with the utmost rigour of the law. The people had been told about it at meetings specifically called for the purpose. According to the statement of a former janitor by the name of Sterrer, the castle had three crematoria. One in the former heating plant, one in the former bake oven, and the third and largest in the courtyard where the drain spout in the shape of a gargoyle is still missing today because it had to make way for the chimney of the crematorium. Since I used to spend my holidays and days off at home next to the castle in Alkoven, I was able to observe the three very large buses being used as a people transport. At peak periods they would drive up three to four times a day, and also at night. During peak periods the crematoria were smoking day and night. Tufts of hair flew from the chimneys onto the street. The bones were stacked on the east side of the castle and hauled away in garbage trucks, first to the Danube, later to the Traun too. Many of the victims were brought in freight cars. The freight cars were left standing outside the Alkoven train station however, and the people were taken up to the castle in buses during the night. Schwarzbauer, a farmhand at the castle, also witnessed a woman coaxing perfectly healthy children from a bus with the words: Come on, children, we're going to see the horsies.

Elizabeth Kramer says, Hans didn't even know there was such a thing as a concentration camp. When Ruth Petzold, that's Hans' second cousin, came on a visit, forty-two, she told Hans, in secret, that they'd taken her uncle. He was head of a ministry department in the Thüringen state government, in Weimar. Hauled him off to a concentration camp, to Buchenwald. Doctor Arthur Petzold.

They let him out again, he wasn't in for very long, but his hair turned white in the short time he was there, that's what Ruth told us.

Ruth didn't talk about it in front of me, I got it from Hans. She said Arthur had to sign a declaration that he wouldn`t tell a soul.

Ruth Petzold says, When this Doctor Frick was made boss in Weimar, he was Nazi Minister of the Interior for Thüringen from the beginning of nineteen-thirty till April thirty-one, uncle couldn't take it anymore.

You only have to look at his evil, shifty eyes, not a very pretty sight, Uncle Arthur said.

They tried to force uncle to join the Party in thirty-three, but he wouldn't. So they put him on leave of absence in thirty-three, at the age of fifty. Then he went into retirement, vegetating away in Weimar. Nineteen-thirty-eight they came and dragged him and his two card-playing cronies away from their little game at the Crown Prince and took them to Buchenwald in a Black Maria, to the concentration camp. When they released him some weeks later at the behest of the Grand Duchess of Weimar, he had to sign a declaration that he would never say a word about it. Months later he told us about it. We had to keep it to ourselves. But I told Hans in Bittelbach. He was horrified.

Elizabeth Kramer says, That's the first time Hans ever heard anything about concentration camps. Forty-two.

Ruth Petzold says, Uncle Arthur's daughter, Charlotte, married First Lieutenant Herbert Wilke from Mannheim, who rose to the rank of wing commander of a Stuka squadron, became a group captain during the war and was decorated with the Iron Cross with Oak Leaves and Swords. His squadron got Rommel out of Africa, him in the lead of course. Back then he gave me an empty cigar box, a foreign one with brilliant colours, which he got from Rommel: To H. Wilke, in gratitude. Unfortunately I gave it away later.

Elizabeth Kramer says, When Hans found out what was going on, he said, I've given my best years to these thugs. But by then it was too late, he died in forty-three.

Thea Langner says, As a child, whenever I went to visit father's grave in the Bittelbach cemetary, I'd always go to see this urn-grave too. When I showed Thomas father's grave in the spring of fifty-eight, I automatically went looking for the other grave without remembering whose grave it was. I never found it. I told mother about it. She said, That was your Uncle Fritz' grave. Then I remembered Fritz Ruttig was the name that used to be on the other grave. My mother also said, I don't know why my parents buried Fritz' urn in Bittelbach. They could have buried it in Kirchnitz, a little closer to Oberlangenreuth.
Thea Langner says, I wrote to the medical director at Zschadrass sanitorium:

I am looking for records and information which will shed light on the medical history and circumstances of death of a relative who was a euthanasia victim in 1940.

My uncle, Fritz Ruttig, born 1905, resident of Oberlangenreuth near Bittelbach, spent several years in a psychiatric clinic in Rodewisch, from which he was supposed to have been transferred to Zschadrass in 1940. That same year the patient's parents received notification of his death, and also the urn containing his ashes, from Hartheim near Linz.

Does your institution still have records, registers, admissions files or the like, which could confirm the temporary housing of patients from Rodewisch?

According to the practice frequently adopted at the time, it may be possible that my uncle died at Zschadrass and that the notification of death was issued at Hartheim as a smoke screen.

Would you know what your institution's involvement was, and what attitude the medical director at the time, Dr. Liebers, had towards issues of sterilzation and euthanasia, and what became of him?

The 75th anniversary volume of your institution, which I got many years ago and have recently got out again, does not, unfortunately, contain any details regarding the period 1933-1945.

Are there more detailed accounts or publications about your institution these days, or would you know of any legal action taken against sanitorium staff in the past?

Possibly there are still older or former employees who would help shed light on my uncle's fate.

I eagerly await your reply and would also be grateful, if you would send me the names of other institutions or persons to whom I may apply in person or in writing.

I thank you very much for your co-operation.

Thea Langner says, I got an answer:

In reply to your letter requesting information about your uncle who was an in-patient here, we may inform you that, according to our records, he was transferred to another institution on 10.09.1940. Which one, is not known to us. We would gladly have given you the information you require, but are unable to do so. Signed, Head of Accounts.

Elizabeth Kramer says, I found an old photo of Fritz. He must have been twenty-two or twenty-three.

Ursula Plog says, His look is full of contradictions. It's on the border between illness and health. It shows in the expression of his mouth: a gentle defiance and a tearful anxiety. It shows in the expression of his eyes, which are both different. One rejects all trust, the other begs for it. One eye watches the other. Sorrow dominates his features. There is no calm in his face. No cheerfulness. There is something of the joker in it, something of the clown. He can't open up to other people. He looks inconsolable. Some desire is still being denied.

Elizabeth Kramer says, Then Karla took really ill. And her husband, Robert, was off in the war. They had to take her from Consbach to Plauen. So they took her from Consbach to Plauen. To the hospital in Bittelbach street.

So Hans, it was during the war, there was no gas, so Hans went and scrounged gas all over the place. Hans said, I don't care, I've got see where I can get some gas, I'm getting Karla out of there. We can't let them find out she's related to us, what do you think's going to happen if they find out, it's dangerous for the children, he said. Said it was a congenital disease, that they're going to investigate and, and one way or another they'll, he was scared, God's sake, he said, don't ever let them find out we're related. We could be in big trouble. He thought they'd sterilize me.

They could have forced me to get sterilized. That's what scared him. He was the one who was scared. It was the law, after all. He already knew all about how they snooped around.

We've got to get her out of there, he said. Karla's got to get out of there, I'm going to find me some gas.

Got her out, too. Found himself some gas and took Karla to a sanitorium in Bayreuth so she'd be out of the Plauen area. In Bayreuth there, that was a private clinic.

He must have fixed it with Doctor Trommer. That was a psychiatrist in Bittelbach. He must have given him letter saying Karla should be taken to the sanitorium in Bayreuth. You could do that. You could always go to a sanitorium.

My father paid for it, I think. Father paid for it and Hans took care of it.

It was a private clinic. Karla always said, Oh, it was so nice there. They were first class doctors, she said, really good to her.

I wasn't able to go visit her, what with small children.

They sterilized Karla in Bayeuth. Because she had schizophrenia. They asked her. If she wanted them to do it. So that she wouldn't have mentally defective children. You have a healthy daughter, after all, a healthy child. If you have another, you can't be sure it's going to be a healthy child, and she should let herself be sterilized. So she said, yes, go ahead. Did they need Robert's permission? But he was off in the war.

With Elfriede, Hans' cousin, it was different. She was a carrier of leukaemia. Went to a doctor who told her, There's something wrong with your lower abdomen, you have to go to hospital. When she got out again, they told

her she was sterilized. Because you would have passed the leukaemia on to your children, Mrs. Schaarschmidt.
Elfriede Schaarschmidt says, I'll be glad to tell you the whole story, only I don't want it to cause me any trouble later. I'd really like to get over to the West one more time. Lonni has invited me to Bochum again.
In nineteen-thirty-three I was operated on by Doctor Burkhardt in a private clinic in Zwickau. I was told I had abdominal growths and a number of other things too. When I came out of the anaesthetic later, I knew what was going on. Of course leukaemia is an awful thing, we had all kinds of problems with my brother. But honesty would have been better. Then I got married in nineteen-thirty-four.

Elizabeth Kramer says, Robert, Karla's husband, committed suicide. Hanged himself. In Badgastein. Just before the collapse. They were being surrounded by the Americans, the troops, in Badgastein. Robert was an orderly. They couldn't even take care of their wounded anymore. They had no medicine, nothing. Robert was a softie, soft as a woman, only no woman's as soft as he was. Karla said, He was a good man. A nice guy. Robert must have known too, that Karla and the little girl had to get out of Czechoslovakia, that they didn't have a home anymore. Maybe he thought, Who knows if Karla and the girl are still alive. He probably didn't know what had become of his parents either. And his sister. He also had a sister in Consbach. His sister and brother-in-law had a laundry. Robert's name was Gradl. His sister married a Lindner. They had a son. They were all evacuated to the west, from Consbach. Karla was in Bavaria too, but went home later with the little girl, Jutta, back to her parents in

Oberlagereuth. Robert was completely cut off. Hanged himself.

George Kramer says, Karla says, Robert died from TB in Badgastein, nineteen-forty-five.

Elizabeth Kramer says, Robert committed suicide. Karla told me so herself. She had it in writing.

Vera Wolff says, Robert Gradl was already a Nazi before the Anschluss, even before thirty-three already; a Henlein-Nazi. My father was in grandfather's shop one day and found out that Robert was getting a few percent commission of every sale grandfather made in Czechoslovakia, even though he never had to lift a finger to get it. He was in a different line of business altogether. Insurance. My father asked grandfather, Why does Robert get a commission? Grandfather, he said, We really sold him a bill of goods, with our Karla there, so we can pay him at least that much.

Robert was in the military hospital in Badgastein and killed himself in the hospital. That's how it was. He was such a Nazi he couldn't get over the collapse. He must have been scared too. Probably thought, Where am I going to go now. Maybe he thought the Czechs, where he lived, were going to lynch him.

Elizabeth Kramer says, But he was no great Nazi. He was too soft.

Karla was sick, a couple of times, during her marriage, and another couple of times after she came home again, to her parents. Ended up in the hospital in Plauen each time. She was never in Rodewisch, she was never that bad.

When Kurt started to have these fits, I got scared. I had sent him to pick up a dress for me on his bike, at the dressmaker's in Obermhlbrunn. He tears straight down the Langgasse but didn't make the curve, so slams right into the curb.

Kurt Kramer says, Father died on the night of August twenty-first, nineteen-forty-three, at the age of thirty-six. I was ten years old. I had to go to Mühlbrunn to pick up my mother's dress for the funeral. On the way back I passed the Langgasse which comes down a steep hill from Bahnhofstrasse. I didn't have my own bike yet, and I always wanted to go down a hill like that. That's why I pushed the bike up the Langgasse, got on it and took off. But mother's bike was too big for me, I couldn't put on the brakes when I got down to the intersection. But I got up again right away, picked up the broken bike and pushed it home. The dress was still in the carrier. Then I noticed blood was streaming down my face. I went into somebody's house and said, Could you put a band-aid on it, please. The people were standing in the kitchen, flabbergasted. I went over to the mirror and got a shock. The people washed my face and put a band-aid over the wound. Then I pushed the bike home. I don't remember the date.

Elizabeth Kramer says, It was on August twenty-seventh. Three days after Hans' funeral. Kurt was supposed to go to Schulpforta in September, to the boarding school. And he comes home with his head all bloody. With the bike, yet. He'd split his head open. His forehead. This wide.

Elfriede was staying with us after Hans' death. She took Kurt to the hospital. Sewed him up with stitches. But they didn't take any x-rays. So Kurt had to go to Schulpforta with stitches in his head, left on the third of September. He came home for the holidays. First holidays of the year. In October. He came home with this huge scar. A fresh scar. We're sitting at the table and there's Kurt going, Heh, heh, heh. He was always fooling around, Kurt was. So I says to him, Come on, Kurt, quit fooling around. Mom! he said all of a sudden, goes to the mirror and keels over. Out cold. God, I thought, now Kurt's having epileptic fits. We put him on the bed in the other room. Kurt was covered in sweat. So I called Doctor Trommer right away, and he came straight over. Looked Kurt over and said, Mrs. Kramer, the head has to be x-rayed.

He got x-rays of the head and said, That's, inside there, that's the scar, the scar's coming into contact with the brain. When that happens he has a seizure, like the one on the other side. If it happens again, they'll have to pump air into the head so there's some air between the scar and the brain.

I'd thought it was an epileptic fit. So I said, Doctor, I got such a fright, I said, You already know there's unfortunately this awful disease runs in my family, is it anything like that?

He said, Oh, Mrs. Kramer, you don't have to worry about your children. Your husband was such a healthy man, had such a positive attitude towards life, all that's been, you don't have to worry about your children. It won't happen. In Kurt's case, it comes from the scar.

The scar grew over. It was fat scar at first. Later it got smaller. Nothing else happened. I don't worry about Kurt anymore.

But to this day I'm still afraid for Thea. After twenty-four years. She had such a bad fall too, as a child, nineteen-forty-three, from the top of the bannisters right to the ground.

Margot, Trudi's daughter, she's been sick quite a lot too. It's in the blood. And with a father like that yet. Harold Heinz. Been drinking ever since he was a boy. Hans told me. Harold had a lot of girlfriends and a lot of children. Hans said, You can't even count the number of children he's had aborted. Harold was no good. Asked Hans what Trudi would get from home if he married her. He asked father for a lot of money, and he got it. In the end, father was just supporting him. But Hans had warned father. Father always held it against him. Because Harold was one of his drinking buddies. Harold used to drink with father, Hans didn't. Never. He just had to go and pick father up in the car all the time. At night, when Hans was unwinding, and tired, father would call and tell Hans to pick him up. In Bertoldsgrün or wherever, ran through all the Grüns around Oberlangenreuth, Irnfriedsgrün, Hartungsgrün. Sat there pissed, and Hans had to pick him up.

Monica, Trudi's other daughter, arrived in nineteen-forty-seven, always was a little, as a child, what do you call it when a child's a little, but harmless, totally harmless. Unworldly. Monica killed herself in nineteen-seventy-five. By accident or on purpose. She took too many of her pills. You really had to pity her in the end. Trudi was dead, Heinz was dead, and her brother Volker and his wife, they were something else. Monica was all alone, had nobody.

She'd trained to be a day-care worker, that's what she was. When she'd had it they put her up at the top of Harold's house. She couldn't get her own furniture, never really felt at home there. Cold and unlived in. She just couldn't cope.

Volker and his wife could have helped support her, he inherited everything from Heinz, after all. There was this Sunday, I went over, eleven in the morning, had a lovely home downstairs, warm, everything nice, but upstairs at Monica's, cold, not properly furnished. I said, Monica, don't you ever cook? Oh no, she said. So I says, Don't you have your meals at Volker's? No.

They could have let her eat with them on Sundays. She worked during the week, in Unterthal, they took care of her there. But on Sundays she was all by herself, all on her own. I thought, No good's going to come of that. Why don't they even care, Volker and his wife. Volker's wife, for her it would have cost too much already, letting Monica have something to eat.

Monica was under medical supervision, had to take these pills. Only she took too many of them.

She gave me a lovely brooch, said, I'm giving it to you, aunt Elizabeth, because you're my mother's sister.

She was a beautiful girl, but was always, didn't have any social life. People who are clever and healthy, they don't want to have anything to do with somebody who's handicapped. That's the way it is. She just didn't have anybody.

(1985)

Sources:

Festschrift aus Anlass des 75jährigen Bestehens der Heilstätten Zschadrass, (VEB Typographical Works Dobeln, n. d.[1969]), 2; 3; 6; 41.

Ernst Klee, Euthanasie im NS-Staat. Die "Vernichtung lebensunwerten Lebens", (Frankfurt am Main, 1983), 100; 352; 353.

Ernst Klee, ed., Dokumente zur "Euthanasie", (Frankfurt am Main, 1985), 104.; Ernst Klee, "Tod und seziert. Bilder eines Albums and die Schrecken der Euthanasie", DIE ZEIT. 40 (20.09.1984): 74.

Hans Marsalek, Euthanasie- und Vergasungsanstalt Hartheim, (Photocopy, Wien, n. d.,[1981]). (Available from the Ministry of the Interior, Federal Republic of Austria).

KEEPER OF THE SHADOWS

A children's story

Whoever came into the shop saw, spread before his eyes, a garden with cobalt blue parrots and purple anemones. Under the trees a brook runs down from the mountains. But he can't see the tops of the trees; the ceiling isn't high enough.

The house where Nicholas Schimmel lived, was old. The garden was older, and Flemish; it was Nicholas Schimmel's Gobelin tapestry. At Nicholas Schimmel's you could have bought a Chinese gong, a lamp of Venetian glass, or a an ivory Christ nailed to an ivory cross with silver nails.

Anything and everything people will pay good money for, that's what Nicholas Schimmel had: pewterware and barrel organs, silver candlesticks, cuckoo clocks, oil lamps, old chests, spinning wheels and rocking chairs. The pewter wasn't polished, and the chests still had their original iron bands with the original dates on them.

Nicholas Schimmel had a sign from an old inn in Würzburg—there maybe was such a place once— and a cradle, only its footboard was broken. He had clarinets, accordions, a zither with no strings, violins, violas, and tuning forks to go with them. He had tobacco pipes, forty different kinds, and hats. He had berets, feather hats, felt hats, a bonnet and an opera hat. Nicholas Schimmel had harnesses, mostly horse collars, long coiled brooms for chimney sweeps, a ship's compass and a dice cup. He had coins, never fewer than two of each so that he could display both obverse and reverse, music boxes, cameos and intaglios, rings, lockets, watch chains, earrings, clasps, and a gold diadem. Nicholas Schimmel had a big shop, shelves took up all the walls, and in the middle stood a counter, half of it taken up by the cash register.

Nicholas Schimmel wrote down everything he had. Anything Nicholas Schimmel wrote down, he put in his desk. And nothing that was written down in his desk was for sale.

Whenever anybody needed anything they would go to Nicholas Schimmel's to buy nails, bird cages, grammaphone records, frying pans, perfume atomizers, keys, mother-of-pearl buttons, picture frames, flower boxes, playing cards, curling tongs, wooden clogs and irons. And just about everything else. But nothing that was not for sale.

Some of the things Nicholas Schimmel had, others had too. But everything, that many another had, Nicholas Schimmel had. And he had all the mirrors.

But Nicholas Schimmel also saw all and knew all.

He saw, kneeling before the cross, someone who had had to go down on their knees, and he wrote the letter that someone had written by the light of this or that oil lamp. He saw the clock and knew who had looked at the time, and he sat at the inn, in Würzburg, ate from the pewter dishes and smoked this or that pipe, his felt hat hanging next to the bonnet which belonged to whoever owned the music box, who also wore the clasp. Nicholas Schimmel paid the bill with his coins.

And anybody could just go right ahead and say whatever they wanted, no matter how simple it sounded, like twittering and chirping. Nicholas Schimmel never said anything; he knew that sparrows and robins and siskins had their language too, and he understood it. That was good enough for him. He had a big bird-cage. Every day he put it out on the windowsill of the window facing out on the courtyard. Sometimes he left it open but the birds always came back, or else it was different ones.

Sometimes a man came into the shop, bought this and that, and stood around in front of the rings and brooches, near the chests in the back, after he had already got and paid for everything. Nicholas Schimmel didn't say anything. He could tell if somebody was just pricing things. The man was about to leave and said nothing, left, and came back another time to see what-all Nicholas Schimmel had.

But no one ever saw all the mirrors that Nicholas Schimmel had. Wall mirrors with painted rims, with engraved glass or frames. Most had wooden frames, with or without ornamental pediments, gilded, one carved, some lacquered. Some had candle-holders. Dressing-table mirrors, vanity mirrors, dainty little cases with comb and scissors and even daintier tortoise-shell mirrors. Handmirrors, beautifully engraved on the back, with elaborate handles, framed in metal, in wood, and again, gilded. Pocket-mirrors, framed in leather or metal, sitting open on the shelf, a cameo on the inside of the lid, or with a delicately chased lid, of silver perhaps. Nicholas Schimmel looked into the mirror and saw everyone who had ever looked into the mirror, and everyone, who had looked into the mirror, had a story. And every story, well, Nicholas Schimmel just has to write it down.

Nicholas Schimmel never talked about his mirrors. Only once, and to a girl who had fallen in love with a wonderful mirror that Nicholas Schimmel had. That's a mirror for a queen, Nicholas Schimmel told her. The girl laughed, Queen! He's sure got funny ideas, that guy. Nicholas Schimmel got things all mixed up; he thought the bonnet, the inlaid music box and the clasp which had always been missing its chain, all belonged to the girl. When he sat at the inn, in Würzburg, he would hang his felt hat up beside the bonnet.

Of all his mirrors, the one he loved most was the one that had belonged to his father. All the mirrors that Nicholas Schimmel had, belonged to him, but this one he called *his* mirror. It was a hand-mirror, set in wood, with a round handle. The frame was painted with wild flowers, the handle too. At the top of the frame sat a bird carved out of wood, singing. But the flower-painter had been able to do more. On the back of the mirror he painted a distant shore with houses on a hillside, and, in the foreground, a blue sea with sailing ships laden down with gaily coloured balls. Nicholas Schimmel's ship's compass had something to do with it, although it remained unclear as to just what. Sure, the ships were big and laden down with gaily coloured balls balls, but whether they were seaworthy; and then the mountains in the background. The houses, perhaps, were Montreux or Rapperswil, the body of water maybe Lake Geneva or Vierwaldstätter Lake or simply a longing for the open sea, which finds it indispensible to have mountains in the background. Mornings, barely awake, Nicholas Schimmel would look into his mirror, see his face and know he was still alive.

The days were already getting colder when two old people came into his shop. The light on his desk was always on. Why do the old people want to sell what the old man is carrying under his arm. It is carefully wrapped, in a black shawl. The woman is wearing a fur collar that has seen better days; the old man's coat, black cloth. He holds himself erect, Take it, he says, the money isn't important, and unwraps what he's got under his arm. The woman helps him, anxious. And Nicholas Schimmel already sees what it is, something he rarely sees. Because he refuses, the old woman says, It's best this way. The children are gone, they used to come to see us sometimes, what do we need such a big place for.

Nicholas Schimmel just stands there, holding the mirror. The two old people can set their minds at ease. He follows them with his eyes. He takes the mirror into the back; it has to be entered along with all the other things in his desk. The two old people, they go home.

Don't look in the mirror, says Nicholas Schimmel. They go home, the two old people, in the rain. The hallway is dark, even on bright days. That's where the mirror used to hang. The old people are silent. The old man goes to his room. In front of his books, with the help of a faint smell of wood from the shelves, he can forget the turmoil in the city, the countless faces, the noise that assaults them on all sides. When it gets darker they have their tea in the big room, at the table in front of the window that looks down on the street. The old man's knees are wrapped in a blanket. Snow mingles with the rain; footprints begin to show on the sidewalk. A smaller flat, a two-room flat, will be warmer. The old people no longer like the high ceilings either. That the thought of moving frightens them, is something each admits only to himself. The mirror was the first thing to go.

Pictures, much of the furniture, crystal, in the next few weeks. That still leaves them time. The children will write.

The mirror is put on the shelf, in the front, across from the counter.

A man who didn't know that Nicholas Schimmel's mirrors were not for sale, or maybe did know, came into the shop and looked around; Nicholas Schimmel didn't know him. It has to be something special, an antique. That one there, he says, meaning the old people's mirror. How much? Nicholas Schimmel is quiet; not that mirror nor any other. That's the one I want, says the man. Here, he pulls out his money. Nicholas Schimmel doesn't say anything. Then the man leaves and says something as he goes, which causes Nicholas Schimmel to fear the old people's mirror.

Left in a hurry, or you would have taken the time, old woman, to pick up the clothes on the floor; you would have put the books back on the shelf properly, your books, old man. And the letters, outside, lying in the snow.

Is that any way to set out on a journey, you won't get very far that way, wrap yourself up in the shawl, and you, old man, where's your coat. The two old people cling to each other in the street, in the headlights of the second truck. The strangers in the first truck are crowded together; there's no room for two more. Into the second truck with the old woman, somebody says.

The old man sits on the black floor of a gymn filled with shouts and darkness, looking around. He doesn't call her name, there are too many people shouting names. He looks over at the door that leads into the hall, to see who's being shoved in and showered with curses. He is confused by the shouts and the searching feet of people looking for other people, who don't see him.

The other truck drives on. More trucks follow behind. Very soon there is no more room for a lot of the people in the second truck. At the door of a gymn the old woman asks about the first truck from her street. Nobody answers her. Nor does she reply to questions about a truck from some other street. All the gymns in the city look alike.

At night, on the floor, all motion ebbs away on the old woman. The woman beside her, who is raving, keeps saying the name of a child she has to find. Before morning the old woman's eyes grow distant. The day goes by her.

Like the countryside she doesn't see on the other side of the walls of the truck.

But the old man clings to his hope. Mats are lying some distance from the door which he no longer looks at. At night he finds room over there. Cautiously, he eats up the bread they give him. Attentively, he follows the orders they yell at him.

He finds a space in the corner of the truck, where he won't be stepped on and where the cold is just the cold. At the end of the trip he searches the faces in front of the barracks. In these strange faces he sees the well-known faces of former days. The damp cold in the barracks is only kept off by the bodies of the men who lie beside him on the plank bed. He doesn't hear the names they tell him. He calls them by the names that he knows. His lips move without making a sound.

Two men who help him up tell him that they have to stand in a line, in the snow. Five to a row. Weak and shivering, they hold him up.

After three hours the snow that the old man sees is black.

As Nicholas Schimmel walks through his shop to unlock the front door in the morning, he sees it, the word painted across his shop window, in white paint. He can read it in his mirrors. Nicholas Schimmel is tired. He doesn't go to the shop door. From his desk he takes out everything he wrote down. He reads over what is not for sale, and in the shop looks over every item written down in his papers. It takes him all day, till well into the night. And not one thing is missing. He reads the stories he wrote down about the mirrors, but there aren't many, and there are a lot of mirrors.

Nicholas Schimmel puts the bundle of papers on his desk and lays his favourite mirror on top. He sits in a big shop, the ceiling is a dome over his head. The walls disappear, and Nicholas Schimmel is left alone. From a tree high up in the dome serrated leaves are falling slowly on Nicholas Schimmel. The leaves sail lower and are blue. The leaves tumble through the branches and are butterflies. The butterflies swim through glass and are violet fish. The fish fall to the ground and are birds.

The shop window shatters and Nicholas Schimmel stands up. He turns on the lights in the shop; the lock on the door smashes. Nicholas Schimmel just stands there. The man who didn't get the mirror, nor any other mirror, is standing in the shop with other men who look just like him.

He goes over to the shelf across from the counter, the shelf with the old people's mirror on it. He says, So keep your mirror, and smashes it against the edge of the counter. The men pull out drawers, hold them at about shoulder height, and dump out nails, buttons, keys. They wind up a music box (Nicholas Schimmel only had music boxes that worked), they pocket coins, rings and clasps, fishing them carefully out of the showcase which someone had pushed in. A man, Nicholas Schimmel recognizes him now, goes up to every mirror except the wall mirrors. Every mirror he goes up to, he smashes against the edge of the counter. He kicks over the spinning wheels and goes over to the chests. He takes pewter plates from the chest, for the wall mirrors. But he leaves one mirror. For that one he takes a violin and smashes it into the glass. Nicholas Schimmel hears the mirrors shatter. He sees the soles of the men's shoes reflected in the fragments on the floor. The men take the bundle of papers from his desk, tear it up and laugh. His mirror has crashed to the floor.

(1971)

FRITZ

Fritz, the boy from a village in Vogtland, who was quiet but happy, who preferred to play by himself, whose dour father couldn't stand him, who could play the piano but never learned, who clung to his mother and had no friends,

Fritz, the youth who wanted to be a pianist but wasn't allowed to, who was a clerk in his father's shop because his father made him, who made deliveries all over the countryside on a motor bike, who fell off the motorbike and didn't love his father because he was a drunk and beat his mother,

Fritz, who didn't want to dress like a clerk anymore, who didn't want to shave anymore, who didn't want to set foot in his father's shop anymore, who just took off over the fields and into the woods and only came back after dark and said nothing, who drove off in the middle of winter with no coat and no money, who was nabbed by the police in München, whose father declared him insane and put him in a lunatic asylum, nineteen-thirty-nine,

Fritz, the man with two different eyes, a light and a dark, a grey and a brown, one suspicious, the other innocent, who was driven insane in the asylum, was classified as a useless life-form and taken to Castle Hartheim near

Linz on the Danube, who was given a gas shower, burned in an oven and sent home to his mother and father in an urn, nineteen-forty,

Fritz, who I never knew, but others told me about.

(1985)

IN THE SHADOW OF A FRIEND

On the last night of October, now that he was finally going to have some fish, suddenly, after eating the first piece, he threw knife and fork on the plate, professing to be revolted by the fish and saying it felt exactly like swallowing poison.

From then on he took only medicine.

The last music he listened to was his brother's requiem.

On Friday he took to his bed.

Actually there's nothing wrong with me, just feel so weak I could fall right through the bed.

The Tuesday after, he thought he was lying in a strange room.

So sing, why don't you, Mr. Bird.

What shall I sing.

And earth proclaim His night, by Johann Ladislaus Pyrker of Felsö-Eör, a generous soul. *The Patriarch coughed up twelve ducats,which was a godsend.*

And earth proclaim His might, you mean.

Alright, alright.

The circle narrows, now he's near. My friend. Rah-rah-rah. As a token of my heartfelt friendship. Vile, the grief that stalks a noble heart. Too light a head hides too heavy a heart. Sorrow sharpens the mind and tempers the soul. Our father and our mother were good to us. Set brow against a common fate. Your Excellency! Rah-rah-rah. My dearest friend!

On Wednesday he let out a scream.
On Wednesday he died.

(1985)

MYLIUS, FOR INSTANCE

I have been dead for two-hundred-and-thirty-two years. But I have never lost my interest in Berlin. I enjoy a good discussion on German affairs. From the distance of Heaven there is much that one sees more clearly, even oneself.

It is easy to say: But for your dealings with Voltaire, nobody would ever have heard of you. But I did have dealings with Voltaire.

Shall I talk about my career? I was promised a professorship in Göttingen as soon as ever I returned from my scientific expedition. To Surinam. But I died before I set foot in New World, even before the Atlantic crossing. Namely in London, of a fever.

That the expedition was a failure, was not in the least my fault. Consentius, who has published several of my letters, had to concede that. At least no one can reproach my courage and zeal with the fact that the enterprise did not end happily. Nor, incidentally, was I lacking the necessary prudentia oeconomica, as Consentius put it. The disbursements I made were all justified. Otherwise I would not have been able to buy even the most necessary equipment. These days, you simply have no idea. I had to pay forty Talers for a pocket watch with a second hand, albeit including the cost of repair; five Talers for a single pair of boots. I was to have, say, six hundred to seven hundred Talers left for the entire expedition. I could not leave Europe on only six or seven hundred Talers, not if I was to be gone for a whole year. It is impossible to accurately estimate in advance how much is required; should an unforseen emergency occur, there is no help where there is no money.

I come from Reichenbach in the Lausitz region. My father was a parson. I studied at Leipzig University. Medicine.

I have frequently been annoyed by the fact that articles about me, invariably brief and rare as they are, always start, right at the beginning, with: A cousin of Lessing's.

It was, after all, *I* who drew Lessing to Berlin. Seventeen-forty-eight. It was through me that my cousin found work with the Vossische Zeitung. February, fifty-one, he even took over my job on the paper. My cousin also lived with me in forty-eight, in Spandau street. Without me he would not have broken with family tradition. His father was also a parson. As a journalist, I was perhaps even his teacher. Thus, for a certain time, it would have been proper to say: Lessing, a cousin of Mylius'.

I am not exaggerating when I say it was harder for me than for my cousin. Only the year I died, he expressed his gratitude by publishing a miscellany of my writings. With Haude and Spener. That I was unable to surmount the difficulties which attend genius in a country like Germany, was due to things my cousin understood perfectly well: lack of even the most basic support, envy, laborious and degrading work. With me it was always I get what I earn, no more. So I had to earn my daily bread if I wanted to live. Was it any wonder that, having sacrificed all my youthful energies, I succumbed to the first serious blow to my health?

After a good two hundred years I am above it all. It is also easier to admit that I prolonged my departure for Surinam because I couldn't help getting involved in the quarrel that had broken out between the President of the Royal Academy of Sciences in Berlin, Pierre Louis Moreau de Maupertuis, and Professor Samuel Koenig, a corresponding member.

I will be brief. Regrettably, I suspect that this quarrel would have been completely forgotten, had Voltaire not got mixed up in it during his sojourn in Prussia, taking Samuel Koening's part. But the quarrel between Maupertuis and Samuel Koenig deserves to be remembered for what it was about, and not for what caused it, regardless of any involvement by Voltaire.

In my defence, I did explain to his then Britannic Majesty's Privy Counsellor and personal physician, the President of the Royal Scientific Society of Göttingen, Albrecht von Haller, that I had been subject to various delays, even though I should have been well on my way to America by then. I said Professor Sulzer had asked me to take barometric and temperature readings in the Harz mines. I really did do this, and spent eight days in the Harz mountains in consequence.

My expedition was under von Haller's patronage. He had also taken upon himself the management of the expedition, including the chief worry, namely collecting the subscription monies and making them over to me.

Another delay was the business with the publisher and bookseller, Martini, who is beneath further notice. As

I see that irksome dealings of that sort are still current today, suffice it to say, Woe to the writer who falls into the clutches of a publisher like this Martini. I hardly ever saw any cash from him.

Nor did it exactly help matters, when the management of the expedition was split in March, fifty-three.

The day after I reached Göttingen on the twenty-eighth of March, I learned that Privy Counsellor von Haller had unexpectedly left for Switzerland on the seventeenth already—for unavoidable reasons, as he left word.

Because a Hungarian by the name of Tekely or Teleky, a Count, who was studying in Göttingen, had insisted on having the hand of von Haller's daughter in marriage, albeit she was to be, and in fact subsequently was, married to a Mr. Günner or Jenner in Switzerland only a few weeks later. As the Count could receive but the obligatory negative replies, he threatened at last to abduct the Miss von Haller, which persuaded the father to whisk her away post haste in order to avoid any embarrassment at the wedding.

Haller was gone, and I never had the good fortune of being able to pay him my personal respects. The money for my journey and all my arrangements for the expedition, he had left with Professor Hollmann. It is not hard to imagine the complexities of a dual management, which I had to disentangle— and all because of some affair of this daughter of von Haller's.

Although von Haller had at times withdrawn his favour as a consequence of the frequent postponement of my departure overseas, I have however the satisfaction of knowing that he valued me all his life.

To him I owe the special honour of having been made a corresponding member of the Royal Scientific Society of Göttingen in recognition of my efforts on behalf of the expedition to Surinam, and other expert contributions. That was in the late summer of fifty-two.

Korff is wrong when he says that Voltaire envied Maupertuis, the President of the Royal Academy of Sciences in Berlin, his privileged position; it sufficed Voltaire that Maupertuis envied him his greater fame.

Maupertuis was a pompous, presumptuous, vain and sinister man who abused his office to suppress free scientific enquiry, and to persecute honest individuals whose only crime was that they disagreed with Maupertuis.

This alone was reason enough for Voltaire to speak out. For Voltaire had an innate need to take the side of the unjustly persecuted.

Maupertuis tyrannized the other scholars; he had Frederick's support.

It was, of course, inevitable that Voltaire would give vent to his hatred of tyranny, and consequently, of Maupertuis.

Is it necessary to go into detail? The cause of the quarrel was silly. But the actions of Mr. President Maupertuis, supported by Frederick, and the manner in which the members of the academy behaved, or had to behave— that's a choice bit of contemporary life.

Briefly: Maupertuis claimed to have discovered the law of minimum force, le Principe de la moindre quantité d'action. Every natural motion requires only the smallest conceivable expenditure of energy; that is, nature is extraordinarily economical. La Loi d'Epargne, he called it, the rule of economy.

But Samuel Koenig of The Hague objected. Koenig acted in the spirit of an enlightened freedom and equality. His reply to Maupertuis in the March issue of Nova Acta Eruditorum contained an excerpt from a letter of the great Leibnitz, wherein Leibnitz expresses himself as follows: "I have observed that, to affectan alteration of motion (l'action), a maximum or a minimum quantity of energy is usually involved."

So Maupertuis' law was no law. It was a plagiarism, and, because it was a bad plagiarism, it was a colossal error.

Instead of keeping quiet about it, Maupertuis did his utmost to silence Koenig.

In the name of the academy he twice demanded that Koenig produce the original Leibnitz letter. Samuel Koenig only had a transcription, which was in the possession of Samuel Henzi. I am willing to believe, now, that Maupertuis was himself in possession of the original.

On the thirteenth of April, fifty-two, Maupertuis had the members of the academy declare the transcription of the Leibnitz letter to be a forgery made by Samuel Koenig. Decision in the matter of Monsieur Koenig, that he is guilty of slandering the good name of Sieur Moreau Maupertuis by means of a forged letter from Leibnitz. The judgement was, for example, signed by Euler, by Formey, sécretaire perpétuel of the Academy, and also by Sulzer.

Euler had even taken a leading role in framing the judgement and read out same to the Academy meeting in question. Whether he was genuinely convinced that the Leibnitz letter was a forgery, I may be permitted to doubt. Euler attached his name out of a hatred for Leibnitz and a not entirely disinterested desire to please Maupertuis.

Euler and Maupertuis were the only qualified specialists in the field, but they ought not to have been party to the decision.

Sulzer has declared that he did not consent to the harsh verdict. That he had no part in it, despite the fact that his name appears on the list of referees. That, because Maupertuis had concentrated all power into his own hands, and open criticism was impossible, covert bitterness against him had mounted, which was doing great harm to the Academy. That bias was evident in all aspects of the Academy's affairs.

Sulzer was not as much of a coward as the rest, and thought it was only proper to give his opinion. He was bold enough to say, and declared with a perfect frankness that does him credit, that he could not consent to what Euler had read out, nor append his signature to such a novel and irregular proceeding for any reason whatsoever.

Most of the signatories to the document held this unjust verdict in abhorrance. How their names and votes were added however, will already have been guessed by anyone with even only a superficial acquaintance of the workings of the academy in question.

Upon a N'est-ce pas, Messieurs?, the entire assembly gave a deep bow, and so the votes were gathered without any fuss.

The world could not know that Sir von Maupertuis treated the full members of the Academy as roughly as a colonel his troops. It was enough that Sulzer forgot himself; Maupertuis saw to it that he lost his Academy pension.

One sees that the unbridled arrogance of this man was bent on toppling by force all great men, living or dead, so that only he would be revered by posterity.

All the same, things were no worse in the Royal Academy in those days than they were later.

Even today one hardly dares to voice one's thoughts in that august forum.

At the time I was ready to believe that Maupertuis would rudely expel Samuel Koenig from the Academy. It was reported, you see, that Frederick had told the Abbé de Prade, a friend of Maupertuis, over dinner, that Samuel Koenig was to be hounded out of the Academy.

This, however, did not happen.

Samuel Koenig quit the Academy by sending his membership diploma back to Maupertuis.

He may, perhaps, have been trying to forestall his expulsion. His resignation would then be so much the worthier a step, as he would, in that case, have preserved the Academy from committing an even greater injustice.

Two hundred years well after my day, the Academy of Sciences did not hesitate to expel respected members who resisted the dominance of the prescribed philosophy and refused to give up the right to free speech.

I am speaking of Mr. Bloch. Who, in nineteen-sixty-two, was deprived of his membership in the Academy under the regime of President Hartke. This has, to use Sulzer's words, done great harm to the Academy.

It is not, of course, my intention to compare Mr. Hartke to Maupertuis, for Maupertuis was, despite his cosmic blunders, a scholar; that is, a mathematician and a geographer of some standing.

Herr Hartke however outdid Maupertuis in one respect: the alacrity with which he carried out orders from higher up against members of the learned organization. And had the insolence to claim that those, like Mr.

Bloch, who contributed to the Academy's reputation, were actually a threat to the Academy's good name.

I am speaking also of Mr. Havemann.

President Hartke, who, as I know, was in the days of the German Führer up to his usual tricks as a member of the Führer's party, read the accusation against Mr. Havemann who was under threat of execution.

Regardless of a lack of the quorum of full members necessary to expel Mr. Havemann, Mr. Havemann was ousted from the Academy.

To get back to Samuel Koenig: Voltaire took his side and, on the eighteenth of September, fifty-two, published his anonymous "A Berlin Academician's Reply to a Parisian Academician," wherein he wrote: "Several Members of the Academy have protested against such a flagrant abuse and would quit the Academy, were it not for their fear of displeasing the King, their patron."

Frederick, Monsiuer de Maupertuis' patron, could think of nothing better than to rush to the aid of the President of the Academy with an anonymous bastard of a polemic, entitled: "A Berlin Academician's Letter to a Parisian Academician."

Voltaire, courageously, and not without trepidation, replied with a destructive attack on Maupertuis in his, "Diatribe du Docteur Akakia," which lampoon it was my honour to translate into German.

Of course it cut Maupertuis to the quick, but there are always new Doctores Akakia waiting in the wings.

That Frederick had the first edition pulped and the second burned by the public hangman in the Berlin Gendarmenmarkt— where the Academy now stands— on Christmas Day, fifty-two, a Sunday, while Voltaire sat in his flat in nearby Taubenstrasse— where he had moved from Potsdam to escape Frederick's wrath— was Voltaire's underlying reason for leaving Prussia.

From Leipzig, Voltaire cancelled his membership in the Academy of Sciences.

I saw Voltaire for the last time on January twenty-ninth, fifty-three, in Berlin. Madame the Countess von Bentinck was also present, and we three constituted an anti-triumvirate, so to speak.

My translation of Akakia, but even more so a street ballad I wrote in a rage over the burning of the book, and which was available all over Berlin the next day, caused me to fear that I might be arrested and put in Spandau. It was thus high time for me to leave Prussian territory, and anyway time to set off on my expedition to Surinam.

De Brunn in Göttingen was of the opinion that the Prussian King would eat me for breakfast faster than the cannibals in America; but I do take it ill on his part, that he added I was just trying to make a name for myself.

Scheidt, the bookseller in Hannover, a good friend of Samuel Koenig's, also warned me never to set foot on Prussian soil again.

I never saw Prussia again in my life.

That my street ballad may once again be read after two hundred years, I owe to Fontius, who found it in the Ponickau Collection in the library of the University of Halle. No more need be said about it.

I will, however, permit myself to recite an epigram I composed on the quarrel between Maupertuis and Samuel Koenig, which still gives me pleasure today:

Minimum Strife

In our much enlightened day
One hears many a scholar say,
Oh, Maximum et Minimum!
From King to schoolboy much ado,
As they all join the quarrel too
For either Tweedledee or -dum.
No end to quarrel is in sight;
Yet ladies, not especially learnèd,
Despite the great name that he's earnèd
With a quantity so slight,
Prefer the maximum by night.

Professor Koenig? He's here too, naturally. Voltaire? That goes without saying. There are a lot of us here.

Maupertuis is not. If he were here, I would know.

Now and again I enjoy the honour of a meeting with Voltaire. He is always surrounded by admirers.

No, Voltaire has never mentioned Madame Denis in my presence. He probably holds it against her, that she sold his library to Catherine the Great of Russia.

He has only mentioned Madame Châtelet. My Emily, he called her.

He has more than once come to speak of his departure from Paris in the year seventeen-fifty, when he left for Prussia, in relation to his departure from Potsdam in fifty-three. He said his flights from persecution were viewed as a betrayal by his persecutors. I did them out of their victim, he said.

What do I read? I read as much German and French literature as possible. Orieux? Superb. In the spirit of Voltaire. Unfortunately he did not mention me.

Germany? Stuffing one's face and swilling are activities apparently still preferred to reading. And one still sees people who only ask, What is he ?, not, What can he do?

But enough.

That I occasionally lapse into an antiquated mode of expression, I beg to lay at the charge of that era from which I spring. Of course I move with the times, but I am a man of the eighteenth century. Is that how you say it?

(1986)

EASTWESTBERLIN

Where does the Qdamm start?[1] The Qdamm starts at number 11. What happened to 1 to 10? The Mövenpick ice-cream seller in the Europa Center Dunno We're from Tauentzien Think the Qdamm starts at the Memorial Church Maybe the Memorial Church is ungodly enough to use up 1 to 10 all for itself

The salesgirl in the foyer of the Memorial Church Oh Lord never asked myself that Have a look inside But the parish office is at 39 Lietzenburger Street

The policeman beside the Memorial Church The Memorial Church doesn't have a street number Doesn't need one either The Qdamm starts with 11 in the war 1 to 10 Just go right in All things must pass It was lemme think 1943 the 23rd of November Christ got his right arm bombed off

I mean There's no door to number 11 But on Breitscheidplatz corner of Tschibo Nanunana Wolsdorf Camelcamel Il pomodoro shirts DM 29 Light-of-Christ Fellowship The New Bible Not a new translation of the

---

[1] Qdamm is a jocular abbreviation of the popular Kudamm, short for Berlin's "strip", the Kurfürstendamm. (In German the Q is pronounced koo).

—*Translator's note.*

Old and New Testaments but the Lord's New Revelation for the Salvation of Mankind available by mail order DM 29 Gyros in pita DM 3.80 The Caravan Seating for 80 Open All Day 10 AM to Midnight Stuffed Aubergines DM 7.50 Bar Live Music Belly Dancers closed for the holidays Checkpoint Charlie House Four exihibitions daily täglich chaque jour The Wall from August 13 to Today Divided Views Artists look at the Wall From Warfront to Gateway to Europe Berlin From Gandhi to Walesa the non-violent struggle for human rights A world-class city with that believes in itself Berlin has its eyes on the future Berlin Savings Bank See The House of Marble is Alive Admittance restricted to 6 years or older Wedding Night in the Haunted House Admittance restricted to 12 or older Poltergeist II Admittance restricted to 16 or older City Shark Admittance restricted to 16 or older Gandhi To all time and change there is a law An enduring and preserving force gives rise to an order that is not mere chance In this I see God

I mean number 11 on the Qdamm first there's the entrance to City Music then the door to Discount Perfumes You wouldn't believe how much cheaper even brand-name perfumes are Nails and Facials and there's the door to Jewellery Showcase precious stones cultured pearls from Japan

TOPgloriasnack 12 Qdamm oven-fresh take-out Open 7 AM Breakfast was never so easy Herr Schott orders a baked potato with sour cream and fried onions plus an Irish Coffee containing four centilitres of Tullamore Whisky Comes to The music is a bit loud Herr Schott says How much I can't hear you The guy with the walrus moustache behind the counter So look at the reading on the cash register Damned if I'm going to yell my head off in here Ten marks says Herr Schott

The Gloria 39 flats will be available in public housing unit Parents responsible for their children Commercial space in the two-storey arcade Restoration of the Gloria cinema

The Colour of Money a film by Martin Scorsese With Paul Newman and Tom Cruise

A young panhandler with rust-coloured curls and long rust-coloured beard sits by the Gloriette showcase

Please Mister Postman clears the mail boxes at the entrance to the Qdamm subway station It is 4:55 Collection times Mon-Fri 8:30 12:15 3:30 4:45 6

A couple is watching a teeny-bopper The man Take a look she's been standing there the whole time she's a The woman You think? But she's still only a child The man So what's she just standing around for all this time then The client And thou shalt be like a watered garden Isaiah forty-eight eleven The girl Lead the way So longs my soul for thee, O God

A bus is parked beside the Qdamm subway station Call 88 42 07 11 Leaves directly from the ZooPalast Big City Tour 11 AM 1:30 PM 4 PM DM 17 Including view over the Wall Mind the regulation sequence Warning shot Second shot Only in this way will there be any substantial improvement in relations between the two Germanies Bus and Boat Tour 1:30 PM DM 27 See the Plötzensee Memorial Holiday Sightseeing Berlin Your Guide Exclusive Berlin by Night 8 PM DM 89 includes dinner son et lumière tour two drinks of your choice Berlin Menu La vie en rose Cabaret consisting of appetizer entrée and dessert West Berlin Supertour 10 AM 2:30 PM DM 22 With a stop at Potsdamer Platz Along the dreamy shores of the Havel River Includes visit with Nefretiti Great East Berlin Tour 10 AM 2:30 PM DM 24 No minimum exchange

East Berlin up close See the original buildings of Berlin Citizens of the Federal Republic must have a valid passport West Berliners a validated visa Unter den Linden the Old Armoury Humboldt University The State Opera The Brandenburger Tor have a coffee the way it was in the good old days Berlin It's Worth Our experienced incoming team Treat yourself to a few magical hours Let one of our fully air-conditioned buses waft you away

Where was number 13 again? Number 14/15 was Pientka. The above prices do not include 13% Value Added Tax 14/15 was also Mampes Fine Dining Wicküler Pilsener ABS braking system (Ashes Bilge Sewage)

Her Majesty's Armed Forces invite all Berliners and visitors to a tattoo From Tauentzien come red uniforms black busbys Pearly Kings and Queens hunting horns bagpipes Blues and Royals The right lane of the Qdamm is closed to traffic A motorist leans out of a car window Go home You're disrupting traffic

Lionel Ritchie stands at the door of City Center ticket booth explaining why he just had to call Brandenburg Country-style Wonderful daily excursions to Berlin's beautiful surroundings in the window The Outrageous Tour ta say Ah love you

Pyramid and Die Morgenpost And above that Bdzko Real Estate A must-see A great buy Tasteful old building with all modern conveniences only steps from Berlin's magnificent Kurfürstendamm Boulevard We offer residential flats locally and city-wide for your own living comfort or as sure-fire rental properties

Don't wait till it's too late Fight the lifting of rent controls Join the Berlin Tenants' Association

Liberals have sold out to property owners landowners and developers

Buy now Or 1995 pay an average of DM 10 per square foot in non-controlled units heat not included in brackets 80% of the flats in old buildings have Dancing on the ceiling

Frühling luxury Hotel near the Zoological Garden offers you every comfort bath shower telephone proprietor

German Travel Agency Entrance around the corner at 38 Joachimsthaler street Children free Free rail travel to Jugoslavia for children up to 17 accompanied by at least one adult We want you to be happy 34 kilometers from Mombassa New house on Diani Beach

Herr Schott crosses Joachimsthaler street and stands before the building at Qdamm 18/19 merkur III Shvayzerland that's the Cafe Kranzler the Kranzler Corner breakfast Merkur coffee quality roasted Swiss Russian tea our specialty Man at the corner table to a woman They said on TV the Russians were treating the Chernobyl reactor like a samovar They're drinking tea by the gallon to help them forget all the fuss Milk Bar iced drinks mixed drinks with crushed ice vanilla chocolate strawberry milk cold drinks fruit juices Mediterranean wines aperitifs whiskies spirits brandy cognac liqueurs Irish Coffee with Irish whisky and German whipped cream Swiss coffe with German Kirsch hot toddies draught beer wines champagne ice cream specialties Souvenir menus only DM 10 Exclusive offer numbered limited edition Cafe Kranzler gold-plated quartz

The talk of the town since 1748 Villeroy & Boch Originals Special offer 16-piece dinner service for 6 DM 569

Herr Schott whose domestic arrangements merely consist of two persons turns to Candy Newspapers and

Souvenirs The Guardian Hannoversche Allgemeine Zeitung The Times Abendblatt Kurier Stuttgarter Zeitung Financial Times Rheinische Post Daily Mail Westfälische Rundschau Sunday Telegraph Die Zeit De Telegraaf Tagesspiegel Neue Presse Stuttgarter Nachrichten Herald Tribune Bild Body sawed in pieces Parts found in freezer Wahrheit Nicaraguan coffee East German candles Comrade seeks flat Daily Express Tageszeitung Oasis of Privacy in Split Brain Sunday Times Frankfurter Allgemeine Hotel and Restaurant News Wallstreet Journal Süddeutsche Zeitung Sunday Mirror Frankfurter Rundschau Le Soir Kölner Stadtrundschau Neue Züricher Zeitung Westdeutsche Allgemeine BZ When millions catch cold the only cure is

Hennes & Mauritz require window dresser for Men's shirt sweater blazer pants DM 253.70 all inclusive Blouse sweater skirt coat DM 247.70 all inclusive The pleasure of making a stylish difference

Do not flash your money thieves are attracted by Reduced fare DM 1 between Wittenbergplatz and Rathenauplatz on routes 19 and 29

Pizza del Arte Open 24 hours Guilt-free dining Gamberetti gratinati con soinaci shrimps on spinach with garlic and topping of baked cheese bechamel sauce Grilled gudgeon with shrimp mussels sauce choron and hot bread Pomodori con mozzarella e basilico and black olives Please ask for our price list We welcome patrons' suggestions

Loneliness makes you fat Boring man seeks boring woman Yawning at home's better when not yawning alone Nationality no object Possible serious relationship

Route 19 Grunewald Roseneck Route 19N Cicero Street Route 29 Grunewald Roseneck

F masochistic sadist (sociologist) seeks M sadistic masochist (preferably psychologist) Thrill-seekers need not apply Codeword Explorations in social psychology

Frullati e panini We use only Italy's finest coffee Illy capuccino for DM 3.50 Just what Herr Schott wants At the door however runs into Herr Knoll senior Hullo Herr Schott Long time no see Member that time Bout time you and I took in another funeral Sure was a real nice funeral

Herr Schott Sure was draws back into the Victoria Arcade ostensibly to go to the hairdresser's gents haircut DM 15 shampoo and trim all inclusive DM 25 complete restyling all inclusive DM 69 ladies shampoo cut and set all inclusive DM 23 A to Z complete hair care girls cut wash dry DM 19 boys DM 17

Knoll has gone Herr Schott looks at himself in the window of the theatre box office Too late for a complete all inclusive restyling sir Why'n't ya go to the live concert with Jamaica Pappa Curvin and Band Four Blacks and two Germans Black faces with white teeth White faces with black teeth What is this thing called happiness Rrrrrreggeggeggeggeggeggae Lowsoft softlow is what happiness is This time is the right time Shit on this shooting pack Shoot on this ruling pack South Africa Afghanistan my Chile and Korea

Attention Smokers Chernobyl is everywhere 250 grams Halfzware[1] only DM 14.50

The Wackersdorf Alliance is holding an information and teaching seminar on blocking regional development through A high radiation count makes hydro consumers

---

[1] A brand of Dutch tobacco very popular in Germany for making roll-your-owns.
—*Translator's note.*

nervous We buy all our groceries where the count is lowest Once we even got a well-known brand taken off the shelves A nuclear Cuba? Send your protest letters against the Cienfugo Montanus nuclear developemnt to Dr. Fidel Castro palacio de la revolucion la Habana Books Magazines Free Nature issue Ecological interdependence in easy-to-grasp illustrations Children and workers contaminated in Scottish nuclear waste plant Don't let your anger cool

Stottrop No way says the girl sew all my own clothes myself

A woman in front of the Hotel am Zoo to a man I'm getting too fat A passer-by Obviously you should get a bike

Ha! Wüstenrot![1] Cute Frenchman seeks room with nice people Gay co-op seeks fifth male

Asterix among the Britons at the Vienna Cinema Men Do it again dad Heartburn

Berliner Runde Beercellar Film production company needs 200 pillows Lend us yours Guaranteed invitation to the premiere Better living through designer living State Porcelain Works formerly Royal Porcelain Works Got all that already What I need's a wife so's the dishes'll get done for once Phone inquiries welcome

Dazzle her with your camera The Pentax Zoom 70 lets you get closer without a hitch The closer the more Motorized focal length Fully automatic from start to finish Flash kicks in instantly With shadow-option Sequentially programmed 10 second delayed-action shutter And last but not least an automatic lens cap that protects the little

---

[1] A real estate firm.
—Translator's note.

marvel from dust Wegert Photo and Stereo That laid-back sound for pampered ears

Hey over here What are you waiting for eh Wanna come with me baby? I really know how ta spoil you Too tired? I'll wake you up don't worry It don't cost much 80 marks for a whole half hour without a rubber With rubber 50 Afterwards you can go home to your wife and rest up I do everything What more d'ya want? Got a cigarette? If ya buy your wife a dinner first it still costs you 80 marks Herr Schott says No

Herr Schott pauses in front of the Bank of Commerce and Industry Qdamm corner of Fasanen street He is only at the beginning of his walk keeping middle and end for later crosses the Qdamm stands in front of the Astor Cinema on the other corner of Qdamm and Fasanen street hears music of George Philippe coming from over the door of Kings Teagarden says Telemann enters the tea shop with 170 varieties served however asks only for 250 grams of Sir Winston's Earl Grey

At the top of the Deutsche Bank Berlin which the President of the German Bundestag is at this very moment entering with wife but no body guards the Christian Science Herald tells Herr Schott that God is all the material world is nought Deny the physical and abolish fear The eyeball's focus can be altered so that one and the same man needs glasses of varying focal lengths

Herr Schott shrinks back makes his way back on this side of the street in the direction he came from Champagne and Fruits de Mer Coffe and Cake Cafe Leysieffer makes its famous Heavenly in the former Chinese embassy Chocolates with fantastically smooth fillings champagne truffle Jamaica rum truffle cognac truffle cinnamon truffle peppermint truffle nougat truffle

Cointreau truffle caramel truffle pistachio truffle mocca truffle Black & White truffle whisky truffle vanilla truffle orange truffle

In the passageway from the Candy Discotheque to the Ho Lin Wah Chinese Restaurant somebody says to Herr Schott I'm Willy Brandt the real one Take a walk along the Wall and you'll get the idea A real thought-internalization process But careful The idea comes from Honecker

Ladies' shoes by Daniel Guccini DM 239.80 by Andrea Carrano by Gino Aldrovani Exclusive Italian shoes Only at Bally

Flights to the USA at excursion fares with Lufthansa New York New York The trip to the city of cities now more attractive than ever Ronny isn't America Henry Fonda would be more like it

Got a mark old buddy?

The Nothing is superior to the Something

The woman Why's there so many policemen running around here The man Because politicians like to walk around among the people these days The people want to bribe the politicians So the police have to protect the politicians

Git yer sausage folks the Russians are coming Got as far as Moscow already

Furs Liquidation Furs Fitchew with Jasmine Mink DM 5998 Saga Pearl Mink DM 9998 Saga Butterfly Mink DM 15998 Saga Cool I Mink DM 17998

Hurry up 'n buy folks b'fore the police comes tsall stolen goods

Aha Berolina Pub Berolina City Tours East Berlin again in German with Pergamon Museum 4 hours DM 29 plus DM 13 guide fee

Herr Schott carefully crosses Meineke Friedrich A philologist and pedagogue died 1870 after all made it to 80

For that real char-broiled taste Burger King Hamburger DM 1.95 Whopper Special with Coke and Regular Fries DM 8.40 The courage of new ideas

Go find a bridge an jump off it Aw lemme alone I'm feeling pretty crazy today

crocodile bags Cherdron umbrellas leatherwear Samsonite luggage bags by Biracci

RubberLeatherVinylS&M Party at the Potsdammer Agreement Potse 67 Admittance by outfit only Come if you don't have a rubber neck

Uelenwinkel is closed Now sir just let Gorbachev get on with it How would you like to wear padded jackets and felt boots all the time They did win the war after all His wife doesn't look so bad either Burda is right If the Russians get something decent to wear and enough to eat they won't have any money left for rockets Only way to have peace Willy Brandt he knew that already Coca Cola that's our secret weapon Here's to Gorbachev You just wait Maybe they'll let Honecker come over too Public enemy number one after all Surprised that Amnesty hasn't done anything for him yet They say he's got a sister in the Saarland Lafontaine he's the only one who really understands Reuniting families

Who controls our life? Hormones at Kurfürstendamm Drugs

Used to have these nice sailor suits at Bleyle's That'd be something for the Russians sir school uniforms Progress through trade

Blue Velvet in the Ufa Palace Who're ya tryin ta kid In deserts or in city jungle Khaki's cool for summer

Teacher with bicycle seeks peace movement environmental activist class-conscious partner with blue eyes and strong commitment against arms race nuclear power and automobile cult

Where it's hopping all week Beer and hot snacks live disco at Joe's on the Kudamm Herr Schott sits down at a table near the door A half The man at the next table Only a half? The waitress brings the beer The man Cheerio! Herr Schott Where did you learn to speak German so well? I was in Germany the last war Where? In Idleberg My son was geborn there Lovely place an't it Next war I'll be back To improve my German But no more wars'd be even better Bad for your health Herr Schott says Yes

Herr Schott continues on his way

People who single-mindedly pursue a clear objective know how absurd lazy compromises for the most part are says Philippe Rosenthal from the show window of his studio building

Sculpture for the Joachimsthaler Platz on Kurfürstendamm by Olaf Maetzels 13.4.81 Concrete iron chrome nickel steel A tower of metal barriers with shopping carts on top Berliners have always been proud of their freedom and tolerance

For lack of mountaineering skills Herr Schott resists the temptation to climb the tower Instead takes his glasses out of his breast pocket to better read the inscriptions Don't pay taxes for this Why get upset about this when you don't say a word about Antes and Wackersdorf Whoever did this belongs in the looney-bin A real corker Whoever pays for this belongs in prison That's what we should do with all barriers We need your support to keep rape-crisis centres open Postal check account number 29 51 96 104 Berlin West Branch number 100 100 10 I merely wish to say that our first-year students could have done better in brackets Metalworking Department That's what you think! But it's not art we support freedom of artistic expression for the people Oh sure we'll all be CDU by and by Just wait and see

Nikon Berliner Kindl Centrtalboden Your mortgage bank Citizen Quartz

Mey has come Only in Berlin do I really feel at home

At the corner of Qdamm and Joachimsthaler Herr Schott startled by the driver of a Yamaha skidding past on the yellow light yanking up his front wheel and revving up on the rear takes a breath Peugeot Mercedes Mazda Audi Talbot BMW Honda Golf Volvo Ascona Nissan Jetta Austin Kadett Renault Kawasaki Scirocco Citroen Polo Taunus Toyota Doubledecker Saab VW bus Ferrari Rekord Lancia Corsa Fiat Lada Mitsubishi Beetle Skoda and crosses Joachimsthaler street with his head down till he gets to Wertheim hears violin music tosses a Mark into the violin case reads I am hungry on a cardboard sign in the right hand of a man sitting on a newspaper and leaning up against a pillar puts a Mark in his left waits on the curb crosses the first lane the second lane passes the Gloria Palace restoration around the Tschibo corner beside Nanunana Wolsdorf Il pomodoro crosses Kant and Hardenberg streets to the ZooPalast it is 2:25 the big East Berlin Tour starts in five minutes Herr Schott is surprised at his speed

At the Invaliden check-point Herr Schott's perfectly valid passport is invalid Herr Schott is not welcome within the territory of the smaller half of the city on account of his birthplace

The experienced incoming team recommends a sight-seeing tour by air from a PANAM plane On flight 640 from Frankfurt Herr Schott flies over the air-space of the forbidden part of the city at 12:50 Herr Schott makes maximum use of the short time to look before the plane veers off to land at Tegel Field 12:55 but can`t hear a thing owing to the noise of the motors

Something yellow shines at Herr Schott in place of the Stock Exchange and Central German Credit Bank Burg street corner of KaiserWilhelmKarlLiebknecht street The Swedish Palace Hotel the citizens' every comfort catered to good service all year round says Herr Schott's neighbour

Behind Kaiser WilhelmKarlLiebknecht Bridge the dome of the cathedral arches up on the right restored by the firm alliance of the National Front for prosperity in town and country Left instead of the royal palace the Palace of the Republic with the Chamber of Peoples' Deputies take part in the work take part in the plan take part in a vibrant socialist democracy

On PalaceMarxEngles Bridge Nike teaches the little boy heroic sagas Pallas trains the youth in the skill of arms Pallas arms the warrior for his first battle Nike crowns the victor Nike helps the wounded warrior to his feet Pallas shields the youth in combat Pallas rouses him to a new battle Iris leads the victorious slain to Olympus beautify our cities and neighbourhoods join in the dialogue between what is rational and what is practical

Behind the bridge to the right the ArsenalMuseumofGermanHistory Permanent exhibition DDR the Socialist Fatherland State of Guaranteedsocialsecurityforaguaranteedfuture with Lenin Memorial in Berlin the final conflict SEDKPdSU on the left the old AcademyofArchitecturethenewDDRMinistryofExternalAffairs sends fraternal greetings to all socialist sister states the world over in solidarity with the Arabian people with the people of South Africa Asia and Latin America in the struggle for the independence and progress of the non-aligned states

The Crown Prince's Palace which is connected to the Princesses' Palace by a walkway over Oberwall street is now the Opera Cafe Disko GrillRestaurantBoulevardCafe

All restaurants in the Opera Cafe require prior reservations Tel 20 71 661 There's always a place for you

Across the street the NeueWacheMemorialtothe-VictimsofFascismandMilitarism guarded by soldiers of the People's Army at all times combat-ready for peace together with their brothers-in-arms daily at 2:50 the small changing of the guard the great changing of the guard every Wednesday Twenty minutes earlier on holidays and memorial days designed according to the plans of a Roman castrum as Schinkel put it

Behind the Neue Wache the PrussianMinistryofFin-anceHeadquartersandHouseofGermanSovietFriendship fraternally onward to the 70th Beginning of a new epoch for humanity 1917

Slightly set back behind it the BerlinChoralSociety-MaximGorkiTheatre Karl Friedrich Zelter died 1832

In the Winter of 1920/21 FriedrichWilhelm-HumboltUniversity had 534 lecturers 12375 students and 2088 special students Today there are over 14000 students at this institution of higher learning building a stronger socialist state through science

The Opera House to the left the German State Opera restored with new

OldRoyalLibraryCabinet on the other side of JosephPlatz-BebelPlatz the great book-burning of May 10 1933 took place under its windows 1945 the facade was still standing The Alexandrov Ensemble sang Wherever I may roam I gryeet the gryeen vallies off home

Kaiser Wilhelm's Palace The Governor's Residence instead of the Niederländische Palais The DiscountBank-theHouseofTradeUnions We do our duty

On the right the Prussian StateLibraryStateLibrary was second only to Paris and London in holdings now second to the LibraryofthePrussianStateArtCollection Do you have a special permit? I'm doing research in Quality and Efficiency

Easier to recognize on the median than in the traffic lanes Trabant Wartburg Trabant Wartburg Trabant Lada Trabant Wartburg Trabant Lada Skoda Trabant Wartburg Golf Trabant Wartburg Lada Skoda Trabant Warburg Trabant Trabant Lada Wartburg Wartburg Trabant

A short hop across Charlotten street Rightleft Bulgaria Meinhardt'sHotelTheSovietBookHotelcafe-VictoriaHotelUnterdenLinden The School of Architecture Affluence we'll make it yet with CafeBauerLindenavenue Friedrichstrasse! NOVOSTI kiosk Soviet Literature Советская педагогика Международная жизнь Вопросы зкономики Колосок Семья и школа Новое ьремя Журнал мод Film Socialist Czechoslovakia Огонек Труд Советская женщина Soviet Woman Soviet Union Неделя Известия Правда

Herr Schott flies over the intersection Rightleft over Switzerland House the Kranzler Cafe ahighriseapartment-theGrandHotel Scandinavian Airlines Meissner Porcelain the French Cultural Centre the Zollernhof the Frei-DeutscheJugend Youth and Thälmann Pioneers forward at the side of our comrades the Balkan Tourist Agency the Neustädtische Kirchstrasse rightleft over the Ministry of Foreign Trade on every continent including Womens' Bookstore the Gallery of Fine Art the second-hand bookstore Fine Used and Antiquarian Books the Cafe on the corner of Schadow street Man with glasses seeks partner with Marxist-Leninist convictions Intourist with Aeroflot office flying higher with top performance Schadow street rightleft over HotelMinervaViratex with the Unter den Linden Gallery the Embassy of the People's Republic of

Poland Young woman seeks adventuresome amateur cook the Russian Embassy-EmbassyoftheUSSR complete insurance for Lenin including the Embassy of the Hungarian People's Republic the MinistryofReligiousAffairsMinistryofHealthMinistryofEducation the happness of our children including the University Bookstore WilhelmOttoGrotewohlstrasse the Brandenburg Gate lost its function when the city walls were torn down in 1865 and is freestanding on both sides

Long live All for The stronger the more Forward At the side Under the banner

over the wall

(1987)